Jackie Col ng writers, with over four hundred books sold in more than forty countries. Her twenty-five bestselling novels have never been out of print. She lives in Beverly Hills, California.

Visit her at www.jackiecollins.com

'A generation of women have learnt more about how to handle their men from Jackie's books than from any kind of manual . . . She seems to know every Hollywood player and just where to find their dirty laundry basket. She is a consummate observer. An outsider with an insider's knowledge. That's her signature trick. She is, at once, both intimate and detached . . . Jackie is very much her own person: a total one-off'

Daily Mail

'Fizzling, sizzling and raunchy from cover to cover'

Daily Express

'Jackie is queen of conspicuously consuming blockbusters about American high life'

Wendy Holden

'Miss Collins knows how to entertain – and that is a very precious commodity'

The Times

'She has a very sharp eye for character and situation'

Guardian

Also by Jackie Collins

The Stud

Drop Dead Beautiful
Hollywood Divorces
Lovers & Players
Deadly Embrace
Hollywood Wives: the New Generation
Lethal Seduction
Dangerous Kiss
L. A. Connections
Thrill!
Vendetta: Lucky's Revenge
Hollywood Kids
American Star
Lady Boss
Rock Star
Hollywood Husbands
Chances
Lucky
Lovers & Gamblers
Hollywood Wives
The World Is Full of Divorced Women
The Love Killers
Sinners
The World Is Full of Married Men

Jackie Collins

The Bitch

PAN BOOKS

First published 1979 by Pan Books

This edition published 2008 by Pan Books
an imprint of Pan Macmillan, a division of Macmillan Publishers Limited
Pan Macmillan, 20 New Wharf Road, London N1 9RR
Basingstoke and Oxford
Associated companies throughout the world
www.panmacmillan.com

ISBN 978-0-330-52140-6

1 3 5 7 9 8 6 4 2

A CIP catalogue record for this book is available from the British Library.

Typeset by SetSystems Ltd, Saffron Walden, Essex
Printed and bound in the UK by
CPI Mackays, Chatham ME5 8TD

For

J. K.

1

Nico Constantine rose from the blackjack table, smiled all round, threw the pretty croupier a fifty-dollar tip, and pocketed twelve shiny gold five-hundred-dollar chips. A nice round six thousand dollars. Not bad for a fast half hour's work. Not good for someone who was already down two hundred thousand.

Nico surveyed the crowded Las Vegas Casino. His intense dark eyes flicked back and forth amongst the assembled company. Little old ladies in floral dresses exhibiting surprising strength as their skinny arms pulled firmly on the slot machines. Florid couples – weak with excitement and too much sun – picking up a fast eighty or ninety dollars at the roulette tables. Strolling hookers – blank eyes alert for the big spenders. The big spenders themselves, in polyester leisure suits, screeching away in middle-American accents at the crap tables.

Nico smiled. Las Vegas always amused him. The hustle and the bustle. The win and the lose. The total unreality.

A carousel town set in the middle of arid desert. A blazing set of neon signs housing all the vices known to man. And a few unknown ones. In Las Vegas – if you could pay for it – you could get it. Just name it.

He lit a long narrow Havana cigar with a wafer-thin

gold Dunhill lighter, and smiled and nodded at the people who went out of their way to catch his eye. A pit boss here, a cigarette girl there, a security guard on his rounds. Nico Constantine was a well-known man in Vegas. More important – Nico Constantine was a gentleman – and how many of those were there left in the world?

He looked good. For forty-nine years of age he looked exceptionally good. Black hair – thick, curly, with slight traces of grey that only enhanced the jet. Black eyes – unfairly surrounded with thick black lashes. A strong nose. Dark olive skin beautifully tanned. A wide-shouldered, thin-hipped body that would make many a younger man envious.

However, the most attractive thing about Nico was his style – his aura – his charisma.

Hand-finished, tailor-made three-piece suits in the very finest cloth. Silk shirts of exquisite quality. Italian-made shoes in glove-soft leather. Nothing but the best for Nico Constantine. It had been his motto since he was twenty years of age.

'Can I get you a drink, Mr Constantine?' A cocktail waitress was at his side, long legs in black cobweb stockings, a wide mouth smiling and full of Las Vegas promise.

He grinned. Naturally he had wonderful teeth, and all his own, with just one vagabond gypsy cap. 'Why not? I think vodka, on the rocks, be sure its 90° proof.' His black eyes flirted with her outrageously, and she loved every minute of it. Women always did. Women positively adored Nico Constantine – and he, in his turn, was certainly not averse to them. From a cocktail waitress, to a Princess, he treated them all the same. Flowers (always red roses); Champagne (always Krug); presents (small gold charms from Tiffany in New York, or, if they lasted more than a few weeks, little diamond trinkets from Cartier).

The cocktail waitress went off to get his drink.

Nico consulted his Patek Phillipe digital gold watch. It was eight o'clock. The evening was ahead of him. He would sip his drink, watch the action, and then he would step once again into the fray, and fate would decide his future.

☆

Nico Constantine was born in 1930 in a poor suburb of Athens. He was the first brother to three sisters, and his childhood had been that of a small boy caught up in a sea of femininity. His sisters fussed, bullied, and smothered him. His mother spoiled him, and various female relatives kissed, cuddled and catered to him at all times.

His father was away a lot, being a crewman on one of the fabulous Onassis yachts – so Nico became the little man of the family. He was a beautiful baby, a cute little toddler, a devastating young boy and by the time he left school at fourteen, every female in the vicinity loved him madly.

His three sisters, not to forget his mother, guarded him ferociously. To them he was a prince.

When his father decided to take him away on a trip as a cabin boy, the entire family rebelled. No way was Nico to be allowed out of their sight. Absolutely no way.

His poor father argued, but to no avail, and Nico was given a job in a nearby fishing port, on the small dock, not a hundred yards, from where one of his sisters worked scraping fish. She watched him like a hawk. If he so much as even talked to a member of the female sex she would appear, bossy and predatory.

The Constantine family desired to keep young Nico as innocent and untouched as possible. They worked on it as a team.

Nico meanwhile was growing up. His body was developing, his balls were dropping, his penis was growing, and most of the time he felt as horny as hell. Well who wouldn't, living in close proximity to four women? His sexual senses were assailed on every level. Naked breasts. Body hair. Creamy female smells. Underclothes hanging up to dry every way he turned.

By the time he was sixteen he was desperate. To jerk off was his only relief, but even that had to be planned like a military operation. Female eyes watched him constantly.

He realised he must run away, although it was a difficult decision to make. After all, leaving behind all that love and adoration . . . It had to be done though. He was being smothered, and it was the only answer. The only way he could become a real man.

He left on a Sunday night in December 1947, and arrived in the City of Athens two days later, cold, tired, hungry, certain he had made a wrong move, and already anxious that his family would come chasing after him.

He had no idea what to do, how to get a job, or even what kind of job to look for.

He wandered around the city, freezing in his thin cotton trousers and shirt, and only an oilskin to keep out the biting ice and sleet.

Finally he took shelter in the entrance of a large apartment building, and stayed there until a chaffeured car pulled up, and two women in furs got out, chattering and laughing together.

Instinct told him to attract their attention. He coughed loudly, caught the eye of one of the women, smiled appealingly, winked, projected unthreatening vulnerability.

'Yes?' the woman asked. 'Do you want my autograph?'

He was always quick, and without hesitation said, 'I have travelled three days to get your autograph.'

He had no idea who she was, only that she was mysteriously beautiful, with soft pale curls, a slender figure beneath the open fur, and a sympathetic smile.

She walked over to him and he inhaled sweet perfume. It reminded him of the womanly smells of home.

'You look exhausted,' she said. Her voice was magical, vibrant, and comforting.

Nico didn't answer. He just looked at her with his black eyes until she took him by the arm and said, 'Come, you shall have a hot drink and some warm clothes.'

Her name was Lise Maria Androtti. She was a very famous opera singer, thirty-three years old, divorced, extremely rich, and the most wonderful person Nico had ever met.

Within days they were lovers. The seventeen-year-old boy, and the thirty-three-year-old woman. She taught him to love her exactly as she had always wanted. And he was a willing learner. Listening, practising, achieving.

'God, Nico!' she would exclaim in the throes of ecstasy. 'You are the cleverest lover I have ever had.' And of course, after her expert tuition – he was.

Her friends were scandalized, and warnings abounded. 'He's hardly more than a child.' 'There'll be an outcry!' 'Your public will never stand for it!'

Lise Maria smiled in the face of their objections. 'He

makes me happy,' she explained. 'He's the best thing that ever happened to me.'

Nico wrote a short formal note to his family. He was fine. He had a job. He would write again soon. He enclosed some of Lise Maria's money. She had insisted; and every month she made sure he did the same again. She understood how painful losing Nico must have been to them. He was truly a wonderful boy.

On Nico's twentieth birthday they were married. A ceremony Lise Maria tried to keep private, but every photographer in Greece turned up, and the small ceremony became a mad circus. The result was that Nico's family finally found out where their precious boy was, and they rushed to Athens, and added to the scandal Lise Maria had tried so calmly to ignore.

Of course there was nothing they could do. It was too late. Besides which, Nico and Lise Maria seemed so unbelievably happy together.

For nineteen years they remained locked in a state of bliss. The age difference seeming to bother neither of them. Only the world press made much of it.

Nico grew from a gauche young male, into a sophisticated man of the world. He developed a taste for the very best in everything, and Lise Maria was well able to afford the millionaire lifestyle they adopted together.

Nico never bothered to work, Lise Maria didn't want him to. He travelled everywhere with her, and taught himself fluent English, French, German, and Italian.

He dabbled on the world stock market, and occasionally did well.

He learned to snow ski, water ski, drive a racing car, ride horses, play polo.

He became expert at bridge, backgammon, and poker.

He acquired an expert knowledge of wine and cuisine.

He was a faithful and ever expanding lover to his beautiful, famous wife. He treated her like a Queen right up until the day she died of cancer in 1969 aged fifty-five.

Then he was lost. Set adrift in a world he did not wish to live in without his beloved Lise Maria.

He was thirty-nine years old and alone for the first time in his life. He had everything – Lise Maria had bequeathed him her fortune. But he had nothing.

He could no longer stand their Athens penthouse, their island retreat, their smart Paris house.

He sold everything. The four cars. The fabulous jewellery. The homes.

He said goodbye to his family, now ensconced in a house in the very centre of Athens, and he set off for America – the one place Lise Maria had never been accepted as the superstar she was all over Europe.

America. A place to forget. New beginnings.

☆

'Here's your vodka Mr Constantine,' the cocktail waitress twinkled at him, '90° proof – not our regular cra . . . er stuff.' She met his eyes with a bold glance, then reluctantly retreated at a signal from a surly blackjack player.

Las Vegas. A truly unique place. Twenty-four-hour non-stop gambling. Lavish hotels and entertainments. Beautiful showgirls. Blazing sunshine.

Nico remembered with a smile his very first sight of the place. Driving from Los Angeles in the dead of night, and after hours of blackness suddenly hitting this neon-lit fantasy in the middle of nowhere. It was a memory that would always linger.

Was it only ten years ago? It seemed like for ever . . .

☆

Nico had arrived in Los Angeles with twenty-five pieces of impeccable Gucci luggage in the summer of 1969. He had rented a white Mercedes, taken up residence in a bungalow attached to the famed Beverly Hills Hotel, and sat back to see if he liked it.

He liked it. Who wouldn't in his position?

He was rich, handsome, available.

He was jumped on within two minutes of settling himself in a private *cabaña* beside the pool.

The jumpee was Dorothy Dainty, a sometime-in-work starlet with a mass of red hair, thirty-eight-inch silicone tits, and an unfortunate habit of talking out of the corner of her mouth like a refugee from a George Raft movie. 'You a producer?' she asked conspiratorily.

Nico looked her over, treated her with respect, and allowed her to show him the town.

To her annoyance he didn't try to fuck her. Dorothy Dainty was amazed. *Everyone* tried to fuck her. Everyone succeeded. What was with this strange foreign creep?

She took him around. The Bistro. La Scala. The Daisy. The Factory. One visit and Nico and the *maître d'* were the best of friends.

After two weeks he didn't need Dorothy. He sent her a

gold charm inscribed with a few kind words, a dozen red roses, and he never called her again.

'The guy has to be a fag!' Dorothy told all her friends, 'Has to be!'

The thought of a man who didn't actually want to fuck her threw her into a decline for weeks!

Nico had no intention of screwing the Dorothy Daintys of this world. His wife had been dead three months, and he certainly felt the physical need of a woman, but nothing would make him lower his standards. He had had the best, and while he accepted the fact that he would never find another Lise Maria – he certainly was looking for something better than Dorothy Dainty.

He decided young girls would be best for him. Fresh-faced beauties with no track record.

He had never been to bed with a woman other than his wife. During the next ten years he made up for lost time and made love to one hundred and twenty fresh-faced beauties. They lasted on an average four weeks each, and not one of them ever regretted having been made love to by Nico Constantine. He was an ace lover. The very best.

He bought himself a mansion in the Hollywood hills, and settled down to having a good time.

The bachelors of the Beverly Hills community flocked around to be his friend. He had everything they all wanted. Class. Style. Panache. The money wasn't so impressive, they all had money, but he had that indefinable quality – a charm that was inborn.

For ten idyllic years Nico lived the good life. He played tennis, swam, messed around on the stock market, gambled with his friends, invested in the occasional deal, made love to beautiful girls, sunbathed, saunaed, hot bathed, went to the best parties, movies, restaurants.

It was a grave shock to him when his money finally ran out.

Nico Constantine broke. Ridiculous. But true. His late wife's lawyers in Athens had been warning him for two years that the estate was running dry. They had wanted him to invest, diversify his capital. Nico had taken no notice – and gradually he had spent everything there was.

The thought of having no money appalled him. He decided something must be done immediately. He was a brilliant gambler, always had been – and the lure of Las Vegas was so very close.

He thought about his situation carefully. How much money did he need to maintain his present lifestyle? He supported his entire family in Athens, but apart from them there was only himself to think about. If he sold his mansion, and rented instead, he would have a substantial lump sum of money, *and* cut his weekly expenditure immediately. It seemed like a wonderful idea. He could take the money from the sale of his house, and in Vegas – with his luck and skill – he would double it – treble it – certainly build it into a substantial stake that he could invest and then live off the income.

Nico had been in Las Vegas exactly twenty-three hours. Already he was down one-hundred-and-ninety-four thousand dollars.

2

Fontaine Khaled woke alone in her New York apartment. She removed her black lace sleep-mask, and reached for the orange juice in her bedside fridge.

Gulping the deliriously cold liquid she groaned aloud. A mammoth hangover was threatening to engulf her entirely. Christ! Studio 54. Two fags. One black. One white. What an entertainment!

She attempted to step out of bed, but felt too weak, and collapsed back amongst her Porthault pillows.

She reached over to her bedside table and picked up a bottle of vitamin pills. E was washed down with the orange juice, then C, then a multi-vitamin, and lastly two massive yeast tablets.

Fontaine sighed, and stretched for a silver hand-mirror. She sat up in bed and studied her face. Yes. She still looked incredible – in spite of the terrible year she had suffered through.

Mrs Fontaine Khaled. Ex-wife of *the* Benjamin Al Khaled – multi billionaire Arab businessman. Actually Fontaine could describe him very accurately as an Arab Shit. I mean what kind of man got away with saying to his wife 'I divorce thee' three times, and then walked away totally and utterly free?

An Arab Shit, that's what kind of man.

Fontaine conveniently blanked out on the more gory details of why Benjamin had divorced her. He had compromised her with sneak photographs of her and a variety of young men making love. It just hadn't been fair. She was entitled to lovers. Benjamin – in his sixties – was hardly likely to satisfy her most demanding needs.

The divorce still upset Fontaine – one of the reasons she had spent the better part of the year in New York, rather than London, where everyone knew. It wasn't Benjamin she missed so much, it was the world-wide respect and security of being Mrs Benjamin Al Khaled.

Of course she still *was* Mrs Khaled, but she made up a neat set of two with his other ex-wife – the one he had left to marry *her*.

Now there was a new Mrs Khaled Mark One. A disgustingly young model by the name of Delores. A very tacky looking girl, Fontaine thought, who was making a complete fool of Benjamin and spending all his money even faster than she had!

To Fontaine's way of thinking the divorce settlement was not equitable to her needs. Her standard of living had taken a sharp dive. She was even reduced to wearing last year's Sable coat. Last year's! *Quelle* horror!

She climbed out of bed, naked as usual. A fine body, full of muscle tone and skin lotion. Firm skin, small breasts as high as a sixteen-year-old.

Fontaine had always looked after herself. Massage. Steam baths. Facials. Exercises. Head-to-toe conditioning.

The work she had put in paid off. Soon she would be

forty years old, and she didn't look a day over twenty-nine. No face lifts either. Just classical English beauty and good bones.

She put on a silk housecoat and rang for her maid, a fat Puerto Rican girl she was thinking of firing if only help wasn't so difficult to find these days . . .

The girl walked into the room without knocking. 'I wish you'd knock, Ria,' Fontaine said irritably. 'I've told you a million and one times.'

Ria smirked at her reflection in the mirrored bedroom. Oh Jeeze – would she like to fuck her boyfriend, Martino, in *these* surroundings!

'Sure Mrs K.,' she said. 'You want I should run you a bath?'

'Yes,' replied Fontaine shortly. She really couldn't stand the girl.

☆

Sarah Grant, Fontaine's closest friend in New York, waited patiently at the Four Seasons for Fontaine to turn up for lunch. She consulted her neat Cartier Tank watch and sighed with annoyance. Fontaine was *always* late, one of her less endearing little habits.

Sarah signalled to the waiter to bring her another martini. She was an extremely striking looking woman, with intense Slavic features, and jet black hair starkly rolled into a bun. She was rich in her own right, having been through two millionaire husbands, and now she was married to a writer called Allan who joined in her tastes for rather bizarre sex. At the moment they were both enjoying an affair with a New England transvestite who wanted to become a folk singer.

Fontaine made her entrance. Heads still turned.

The two women kissed, mouths barely brushing each other's cheeks.

'How was Beverly Hills?' Fontaine demanded. 'Did you have a divine time?'

Sarah shrugged, 'You know how I feel about Los Angeles. Boring and hot. Allan enjoyed it though, someone has finally been fool enough to option his screenplay. They paid him twenty thousand dollars. You would think he had personally discovered gold!'

'How sweet.'

'Adorable. My man has money at last. It will just about cover one quarter's payment on my jewellery insurance!'

Fontaine laughed, 'Sarah, you're so mean . . . The poor man has balls, you know.'

'Oh yes? *Do* tell me where he keeps them. I'd simply *love* to know.'

Lunch passed by in a flurry of the latest gossip – both women were experts. By the time coffee arrived they had carved up everyone and anyone, and loved every minute of it.

Sarah sipped her Grand Marnier, 'I saw an old friend of yours on the Coast,' she said casually. 'Remember Tony?'

'Tony?' Fontaine feigned ignorance, but she knew immediately who Sarah was talking about. Tony Blake. Tony the stud.

'*He* remembers *you*,' Sarah mocked. 'And with a quite violent lack of affection. What *did* you do to him?'

Fontaine frowned, 'I took him from being a nothing

little waiter, and built him into the best manager of the best discothèque in London.'

'Oh yes. Then you threw him out, didn't you?'

'I dispensed with *his services* before *he* dispensed with mine. The cocky little bastard was only trying to open up on his own, knock me out of business.'

Sarah laughed, 'So what happened?'

'I thought I told you all about it. *I* went partners with his money man before *he* could. Poetic justice. I haven't heard from him since. What *is* he doing in LA?'

'Sniffing, snorting, what everyone does in LA. By the way, whatever happened to your club, "Hobo" wasn't it?'

Fontaine extracted an art deco compact from her Vuitton purse and minutely studied her face. 'My club is still going strong, still *the* place.' She selected a small tube of lip gloss and smoothed it over her lips with her finger. 'As a matter of fact I had a letter from my lawyer this morning. He seems to feel I should be getting back, sort out my affairs.'

'And *what* affairs are those?' Sarah teased.

Fontaine snapped the compact shut. 'The monetary kind darling. They're the only kind that matter aren't they?'

☆

After the lunch they parted and went their separate ways. Fontaine felt that she had to keep up a certain front, even with a close friend like Sarah. As she strolled along Fifth Avenue she thought about the letter from her lawyer and what it had *really* said. Financial difficulties . . . Unpaid bills . . . Spending too much money . . . 'Hobo' in trouble . . .

Yes, the time had certainly come to return to London and sort things out.

But how could 'Hobo' possibly be in trouble? From the moment Benjamin had bought the place for her it had made money. Tony – her manager – lover – and stud – had become the most wanted man in London when she had put him in charge. And when she had got rid of him – Ian Thaine, her new partner – had redecorated the place, put in a new manager, and then got pissed off because she was not prepared to extend the partnership on to a personal level. So she had bought him out, and when she had left London 'Hobo' had been flourishing. And it was all hers, and should be a substantial asset; not a goddamn drain on her finances.

It was starting to rain, and Fontaine looked around in vain for a cab. God! It was about time she found herself another millionaire – who needed this searching for cabs garbage – she should have a chauffeur-driven Rolls, as she had always had when she was Mrs Benjamin Khaled. As it was she could only afford to hire a limousine and chauffeur for the evenings. She needed it desperately then, as the escorts she chose barely owned more than a motorbike – if that. Fontaine liked the men in her life to keep their assets on show – right up front – in their trousers.

She had never really pursued money, because of her devastating beauty it had always managed to pursue her. Benjamin Al Khaled for instance had spotted her when she was modelling in a St Moritz fashion show and dumped his first wife quicker than a hooker gives head.

After life with Benjamin, money was a necessity. Fontaine had a taste for the best that was very hard to quench.

But she had wanted a pause before searching out another billionaire husband. Billionaire equalled old (unless you counted the freaked-out rock stars who always seemed to tie themselves up with young blonde starlets anyway). And old was not what Fontaine needed. She needed youth – she enjoyed youth – she revelled in the male body beautiful and an eight- or nine-inch solid cock.

A drunk weaved across Fifth Avenue and planted himself swaying and dribbling in front of her, blocking her path. 'Ya wanna get laid?' he demanded, displaying a mouthful of leer.

Fontaine ignored him, attempted to pass.

'Hey,' he managed to obstruct her way. 'Wassamatter? You don' wanna fuck?'

Fontaine gave him a hard shove, saw a cab, ran for it, collapsed in the back and sighed.

It really was time to get out of New York.

☆

The very moment Fontaine departed for her lunch date, Ria, her Puerto Rican maid, rushed for the phone. Ten minutes later her boyfriend arrived. Martino. The best looking black guy in the whole of fuckin' New York City.

'Whatcha say, babe?' He greeted her with a kiss and a goose, while his stoned eyes checked out every inch of the luxurious apartment.

'We got two hours,' Ria said quickly. 'The bitch won't be back before that.'

'Let's go then, babe, let's go.'

'Sure, hon. Only thing is . . . Well I got me a fantasy. Martino, can we waste five whole minutes? Can I show you her bedroom? Can we make it all over her crazy fuckin' bedroom?'

Martino grinned. He was already unzipping his shiny leather pants.

☆

Fontaine spent the afternoon at the beauty parlour listening to more gossip. Some of it was a repeat of what Sarah had already told her, but it was interesting to have it confirmed.

'I'm going back to London,' Fontaine confided to Leslie, her hairdresser.

'Yeah?' Leslie grinned, he had nice teeth, a good face, a nice body, but he was minus where he should be plus – a fact that Fontaine had personally checked.

'It's about time I had a change of scenery,' Fontaine continued. 'I feel as though I'm getting too static here.'

'I know what you mean,' Leslie replied sympathetically. Christ! Fontaine Khaled getting static! That was a laugh. The old bitch must have balled everything under twenty-five that walked in New York City!

Leslie himself was twenty-six, and not pleased that the notorious Mrs Khaled had taken him to bed only once, and then abandoned him like a bad smell. Oh, he was still all right to do her hair – and why not – he was the best goddamn hairdresser in town. The most fashionable too.

'Will you miss me, Leslie?' Fontaine fixed him with her lethal kaleidoscope eyes.

She was flirting and Leslie knew it. *What's the matter Mrs Khaled? Got a few hours to fill?*

'Of course I'll miss you, every time I set a wig I'll remember you!'

Game set and match to Leslie. For a change.

☆

Fontaine was not in a good humour when she returned to her apartment. The horrible man in the street. Leslie getting smart ass. And then a foul-smelling cab driver who insisted on discussing President Carter's piles – as though they were a serious part of political history. Cretin! Asshole! And she had a headache too.

Going up in the elevator she didn't bother to search for her key. She rang the doorbell, and cursed when it took Ria forever to answer.

It finally occurred to her that the stupid girl wasn't going to come to the door at all. She was probably asleep, slouched over a soap opera on television.

Furious, Fontaine rifled through her bag for her Gucci keyring, found it, and let herself into the apartment with an angry commanding shout of – 'Ria! Where the *hell* are you!'

The sight that greeted her eyes was not a pretty one. Her apartment had been stripped, and from what she could see at first glance, what had been left was wrecked.

Shocked, she took two steps inside, and then realizing that Ria might be lying mutilated and murdered amongst the debris, or even that the robbers might still be on the premises, she backed quickly out.

☆

The police were very good. It only took them an hour and a half to arrive, and they discovered no murdered Ria, just 'Fockin' Beetch!' scrawled in lipstick all over the mirrored bedroom.

Fontaine recognized the scrawl as being Ria's illiterate scribble.

Everything that could be moved was gone. Her clothes, luggage, toiletries, sheets, towels, small items of furniture – even light fitments and all electrical gadgets including the vacuum that Ria had pushed so disdainfully around the apartment.

The bed, stripped of everything except the mattress, bore its own personal message – a congealing mess of sperm.

'God Almighty!' Fontaine was fuming. She glared at the two patrolmen. 'Where the hell's the detective that is going to investigate this case? I have *very* important friends you know, and I want some action – fast!'

The two cops exchanged glances. Let's hope to Christ they don't put Slamish on this case they both thought at the same time. But they both knew it was inevitable. Slamish and Fontaine were destined to meet.

☆

Chief Detective Marvin H. Slamish had three unfortunate things going for him. One – an uncontrollable defect in his left eye that caused him to wink at the most inopportune moments. Two – a tendency to store wind, and never to be quite sure when it would emerge. Three – a strong body odour that no amount of deodorants could smother.

Chief Detective Marvin H. Slamish was not a happy man.

He used mouthwash, underarm roll-ons, powders and sprays, and female vaginal deodorants sprayed liberally over his private parts.

He still smelled lousy.

Fontaine sniffed the moment he entered her apartment, 'My God! What's that terrible smell?'

Chief Detective Marvin H. Slamish winked, farted and removed his raincoat.

Fontaine was unamused. She gestured around her looted apartment, 'What are you going to do about this?' Her voice zinged with English authority. She glared at Chief Detective Slamish as though it was his own personal fault. 'Well?' her kaleidoscope eyes regarded him with disdain. 'Have you found my maid yet?'

Chief Detective Slamish slumped into a remaining chair, the stuffing bulging from where it had been ripped open. He had not had a good day. In fact his day had been pure shit. A drug bust that hadn't stuck. A row with his one-armed Vietnam-war-veteran brother-in-law who was the biggest con artist in Manhattan. And now this stiff-assed English society broad. Wasn't it enough that his balls ached? Wasn't it enough that his strong odour was beginning to pervade even his insensitive nostrils?

'Everything's under control ma'am,' he mumbled unconvincingly.

'Under control?' Fontaine arched incredulous eyebrows. 'Have you recovered my property? Have you arrested my maid?'

The two cops exchanged glances.

Slamish tried to summon an air of confidence and authority. 'Just give us time, ma'am, just give us time. An investigation is getting under way right now. In fact there are a few questions I'd like to ask you.'

'Questions? Me? You have to be kidding. *I'm* not the criminal in the case.'

'Of course you're not, ma'am. But then again it hasn't been unheard of for people to er . . . arrange things. Insurance . . . You know what I mean?'

Fontaine's eyes blazed. 'Are you implying that I might have set this up myself?'

It was an unfortunate moment for Slamish to wink.

'You *horrible* little man!' Fontaine screamed. 'I'll have your badge for your . . . your impertinence!'

Wearily Slamish rose, farted, and attempted to apologise.

'Get out of here,' Fontaine stormed. 'I don't want you on my case. My husband is Benjamin Al Khaled and when I tell him of your accusations . . .'

Chief Detective Slamish headed for the door. Some days it just wasn't worth getting out of bed.

☆

Five long hours later Fontaine was comfortably installed in a suite at the Pierre Hotel. Thank God the bastards hadn't taken her jewellery. It had been safely locked up at the bank – a precaution Benjamin had always insisted on, and one that she had followed through with.

As for the apartment – well it had needed decorating. And her clothes . . . A new wardrobe was never a problem, and fortunately she was adequately insured.

Yes. A couple of days at the Pierre while she got herself together and did some shopping.

Then home . . . London . . . 'Hobo' . . . And a sorting-out of her life.

3

Bernie Darrell had been divorced four months, two days and twelve hours exactly. He knew, because his ex-wife, Susanna, never tired of telephoning to let him know. Of course there were other reasons she telephoned. The pool was malfunctioning. Her Ferrari had broken down. Their child missed him. Was he really tasteless enough to be seen at 'Pips' – a Beverly Hills discothèque – with another woman? So soon? How did he think she felt?

God! He would never really understand women. Susanna and he had spent a miserable five years as a married couple – in spite of how the gossip columns and fan magazines built them up as love's young dream.

Susanna Brent, beautiful young actress daughter of Carlos Brent, the famed singer/movie star/rumoured mafioso. And Bernie Darrell – hot shot record company mogul.

Mogul! Him! That was a laugh! He had managed to keep Susanna in the style to which she was accustomed. Just. Only just. And she had never tired of throwing daddy in his face, and how much better he could do it.

One morning Bernie had packed a suitcase, stacked it in the back of his silver Porsche, and fled. Susanna had been begging him to come back ever since.

Bernie didn't have much sense, but with the counsel of his friends, he had realised that to go back was to present Susanna with his *balls* – on a plate – nicely garnished. The longer he stayed away, the more he knew this to be the truth.

He was lucky to have a friend like Nico Constantine. Nico had allowed him to move into his house with an invitation to stay as long as he wanted. So far he had stayed seven months, and enjoyed Nico's company so much that he had no desire to find a place of his own.

Nico was his idol. He was everything that Bernie aspired to be. Bernie copied him religiously, but the result was not yet perfect.

At twenty-nine years of age Bernie had youth on his side. He was slim and athletic, and did all the good things such as tennis, jogging, working out at a gym. He also smoked grass profusely, sniffed coke constantly, and drank like a new generation Dean Martin.

Nico didn't touch drugs, and Bernie vowed he would give them up. But it was always tomorrow as far as he was concerned . . . and he never seemed to get around to tomorrow. Anyway he *needed* drugs, it was a social politeness. I mean as boss of a West Coast record company, how could he sit around at a meeting with one of his groups and not indulge? Professional murder. They would move on faster than a fag at an Anita Bryant coffee clutch.

Bernie attempted to imitate Nico's style of dress, but the suits were never that immaculate fit that Nico so effortlessly achieved, the shirts never laid correctly around the collar – even the hand-made ones. He looked good, but only until he stood next to Nico.

Bernie had a handsome bland face, capped teeth, bad breath, permed hair, a scar on his stomach, a perfect permanent suntan, and a small penis.

One of the great things about Susanna was that in all their mud-slinging arguments she had *never* mentioned his little dick. Never. He loved her for that.

Now Bernie sat on a Las Vegas-bound plane, staring out of the window, wondering how the *hell* he was going to explain Cherry to Nico.

Cherry sat beside him, elegant hands crossed primly on her lap. Beautiful face in repose. Long straight blonde hair hanging luxuriously down.

She was a knockout. Nico's knockout to be precise. He had dumped her a week ago with the roses, and the diamond trinket, and the usual speech about how he was only leaving her for her own good – and how much happier she would be without him.

What a bullshit artist Nico was. The absolute best. The original fuck-and-run merchant. He always left the girl thinking *she* had left him! Clever.

In seven months Bernie had seen him do it to six of them. All staggeringly beautiful in that newly scrubbed, wholesome young way. They all left without a whimper. Nico was right, they *would* be better off without him, (quite why they never seemed to figure out) but they parted the best of friends, and wore his diamond trinket from Cartier (usually a mouse or a butterfly) and spoke about him in only the most glowing of terms.

Bernie had never had that kind of luck with women. Whenever he tried to dump a girl they had hysterics, called him a motherfucking son-of-a-bitch bastard, and badmouthed him all over town.

What was he doing wrong?

'How long before we land?' Cherry asked sweetly.

Oh Christ! Cherry. She had turned up at the house looking for Nico. And she had been there when Nico had phoned from Las Vegas telling Bernie to grab some money and get on the next plane out. Then, firmly, but of course with bags of innocent girlishness, she had insisted on coming too. 'I have to talk with Nico,' she explained. 'My life is at a crossroads, and only he can help me.'

'Can't you wait a coupla days?' Bernie had grumbled, 'He'll be back in LA before that.'

'No. I have to see him immediately.'

So he had been unable to shake Cherry. And what *really* bugged him was she had let *him* pay for her ticket. The nerve! Not one move towards her purse, just a sweet smile, a soft hand on his arm and a 'Thank you, Bernie.'

Of course everyone thought he was loaded. If he didn't know better he would think so himself.

The newspapers described him as Bernie Darrell, millionaire record boss. Well the company did OK. But millionaire? Forget it He could barely scrape enough together to make Susanna's ludicrous alimony payments. And of course, being Carlos Brent's son-in-law – even though he was ex-son-in-law – meant always having to pick up the check.

He wondered what Nico had meant by 'grab some money'. It seemed like such a strange request coming from Nico. Nico was always very flush, always the big spender. And in Vegas surely he could get as much credit as he could use? Anyway, Bernie had stopped by his office and extracted six thousand cash from his safe. It occurred to him that ever since moving in with Nico he had never made an attempt to pay one household account. Even the liquor he ordered at the corner store and had them bill it to the house. He felt a bit guilty now, but Nico was truly the perfect host, and never expected a guest to put his hand in his pocket – even a seven-month guest.

Somewhere in the back of his mind Bernie knew that maybe something was amiss financially for Nico. A series of events pointed to this. Firstly, why had Nico suddenly sold his house two months previously? He had got a good price, but everyone knew that if you had Beverly Hills real estate the name of the game was to sit on it. Prices were escalating at an exciting rate.

Bernie had joked at the time, 'Trying to get rid of a difficult house guest, huh?'

Nico had smiled that enigmatic smile of his, and made all arrangements to move them over to the new house he had rented. No discomfort for anyone.

Then another thing Bernie had noticed, stacks of unpaid bills were starting to accumulate on Nico's desk, and Nico had always been meticulous at settling his accounts immediately.

Just little things, but enough to make Bernie wonder somewhere in the back of his mind – a place he didn't visit too often.

Cherry said, 'Ooops! I'm not too fond of landings.'

She looked a little green. Bernie handed her the paper bag to throw up in, and sat back to enjoy the descent.

☆

Nico had no sense of time. He had been sitting at the baccarat table how long? Two, three, four hours? He just didn't know. He only knew that the losing streak he was on had no intention of quitting.

A thin film of sweat skirted his brow, but otherwise he was unaffected – his usual smiling charming self.

His plan had gone disastrously horribly wrong. What had started out as a fool-proof scheme to make a big killing – had turned into a joke. He had lost every single dollar he had made on his house – worse – he had gone beyond that – and was now into the Casino for five hundred thousand dollars.

So much for skill and talent and luck. If the cards and dice were against you there was simply nothing you could do. Except stop playing. And he hadn't done that. He had kept right on going like some schmuck from the sticks.

He was now in a far more difficult situation than merely being broke. He was in debt to people who were hardly likely to be thrilled when they found out he couldn't pay up.

It was like a bad dream. It seemed to have happened before he knew it.

Two days. That's all it had taken.

The woman sitting beside him was pushing the baccarat shoe towards him. She was winning, quite heavily, and flirting with Nico, although she must have been well on her way towards being sixty. Her chubby arms and fingers were garnished liberally with jewellery, quite incredible jewellery – tasteless but effective. On her left hand she wore a gigantic diamond. Nico was fascinated by the size of it. It had to be worth at the very least five hundred thousand dollars.

☆

As the cab took him and Cherry from the airport, Bernie was disgusted to see that Carlos Brent himself was headlining at 'The Forum Hotel'. Why the hell had Nico picked there?

'I've never been here before,' Cherry remarked, smoothing down her skirt with delicate pale hands.

'Don't get too comfortable,' Bernie muttered, 'you may be on the next plane back.'

'I don't think so,' replied Cherry, primly.

Oh yeah? One thing Bernie knew about Nico was that once a broad was out she was out. No going back, however golden the muff.

Bernie was greeted regally at the reception desk. As Carlos Brent's ex-son-in-law he was a well-known figure at the Forum. He and Susanna had spent part of their honeymoon there – they had had to, Carlos was appearing at the time and he had insisted that the whole goddamn wedding party flew back to Vegas with him to celebrate.

Shit! Making love to his new bride with her famous daddy in the adjoining penthouse suite had not been the greatest of experiences.

'I'd like to freshen up before I see Nico,' Cherry was saying.

'Yeah,' Bernie agreed. 'Give me the key to Nico Constantine's suite,' he told the girl behind the desk. 'It'll be fine, he's expecting us.'

'Certainly Mr Darrell,' she said, giving Cherry a quick once-over from head to toe. News would have filtered over to Carlos that Bernie had arrived in Vegas with a nineteen-year-old blonde within the hour.

'This is Miss Cherry Lotte,' Bernie said quickly. 'Mr Constantine's fiancée.' Fiancée! Sweet! What a lovely old-fashioned word! Nico would kill him. But it was better than having Carlos Brent pissed off.

☆

The baccarat shoe was emptied of cards by the bejewelled woman. Pass after pass she, won, until the shoe was finished. She sorted out her stacks and stacks of chips with fat hands, and Nico was once again mesmerized by the size of her diamond ring.

He stood up. The pit boss said, 'Staying for another shoe Mr Constantine?'

Nico forced a smile as he left the enclosure, 'I'll be back later.'

He felt sick to his stomach, and then he saw Bernie hurrying towards him, and his spirits lifted. Bernie would have a way to bail him out. Bernie was a sharp kid, and anyway – after seven months of free everything he owed him a favour.

☆

On the very top floor of the Forum Hotel, Joseph Fonicetti kept his eye on the proceedings. He owned the Forum, and with the help of his two sons, Dino and David, he ran a tight ship. Not too much happened within the confines of the Forum that Joseph Fonicetti didn't know about.

For instance – the fourth girl on the right – back chorus line – had obtained an abortion the previous afternoon. She would be back at work tonight.

For instance – two waitresses in the Orgy Room were stealing – nickel-and-dime stuff. Joseph would keep them on, good waitresses were hard to find.

For instance – one of his pit bosses was planning to screw the Casino manager's wife. That would have to be stopped – immediately.

'What about Nico Constantine?' David asked his father.

'How much is he in to us for now?' Joseph replied, his eyes flicking across his four closed-circuit TV screens that showed him plenty of action.

David picked up a phone to get up-to-the-minute information.

'He's given us six hundred thousand of his money – and he's into us for five hundred and ten thousand. He just left the baccarat table and is meeting with Bernie Darrell.'

'I like Nico,' Joseph said softly. 'But no more than another fifty thousand credit, and see that he pays us before he leaves Vegas. You take care of it, Dino.'

'Do we take a cheque?' Dino asked.

Joseph closed his eyes, 'From Nico? Sure. Nico has plenty of money. Besides, he's too smart to ever try to shaft us. Besides, Nico Constantine without his balls – what kind of a ladies' man would that be?'

4

Fontaine zipped through the New York stores at an alarming pace. When it came to shopping for clothes there was nobody better at spending money than she was – except perhaps Jackie Onassis.

She used her credit cards liberally, unworried by the fact that her lawyer in England had warned her to run up absolutely no more bills.

She had been robbed. Surely she was entitled to clothe herself for her imminent return to London?

Armani, Cerrutti, Chloe – name-designer clothes had always looked well on her.

She had lunch with Allan Grant, Sarah's husband. He amused her, wanted to take her to bed for the afternoon. She demurred. She had so much more shopping to do. And she was to depart for London the very next day. She really didn't want to hurt Allan's feelings, she had been to bed with him before, but he was simply not her style. At thirty-six he was too old for her. Why settle for an old model when you could have the very latest twenty-two-year-old actor with a body like a young Marlon Brando?

Fontaine had always been a puller supreme. Men could never resist the lure of her perfumed thighs. Besides which, she had that very rare commodity – good old-fashioned glamour – and men – especially young men – loved it.

She left Allan, and went shopping in Henri Bendels, where she bought two pairs of boots at a hundred and eighty-five dollars apiece. A simple black crocodile shoulder bag – four hundred dollars. An art deco necklace and earrings – one hundred and fifty dollars. And three hundred dollars' worth of make-up and perfume.

She charged everything, and ordered it sent special delivery to her hotel. Then she decided that she really must get some rest before the evening's activities, and she took a taxi to the Pierre, where she had a long luxurious bubble bath, carefully applied a special cucumber face mask, and went to sleep for three and a half hours.

☆

Jump Jennings checked out his appearance one more nervous time before leaving his seedy village apartment. He looked good, he knew *that*. But the question was – did he look good enough? Tonight was the night to find out.

Jump had been christened Arthur George Jennings, but he had been nicknamed Jump in high school because of his athletic prowess, and it had just sort of stuck. Jump wasn't a bad name to be stuck with either. Jump Jennings. It sounded pretty good. It would *look* pretty good one day – stuck up on a marquee in lights next to Streisand or Redford. Rock, Tab, Rip . . . The world would be ready for Jump. His time would come. He hoped desperately that his time would come that very night.

He hitched up his black leather trousers, and adjusted

the collar of his black leather bomber jacket. Sylvester Stallone was the look. Yeah – and it suited him too.

Confident at last, he left the apartment.

☆

Fontaine awoke an hour before her date was due to pick her up. There was an exciting evening ahead. An art gallery opening, two parties, then the inevitable Studio 54 – a wild huge discothèque where anything could happen, and usually did.

She dressed with care after applying an impeccable makeup. She wore a deeply V-necked brown satin wrap dress, tightly belted over narrow crêpe de chine trousers. Strappy high-heeled pewter sandals by Halston completed the look.

One of Leslie's juniors arrived to comb out her hair and by the time he was finished teasing and crimping, she looked a knockout.

Of course her diamonds and emeralds helped. They always did.

Jump Jennings turned up on time. Fontaine shuddered at his choice of outfit. He looked like a refugee from the Hells Angels. Would her friends laugh? After all there was such a thing as going too far.

'Don't you have a suit?' she asked rather testily.

'Wassamatter with the leather?' Jump questioned aggressively.

It's very . . . macho. But a suit might be more . . . well *right*. Something Italian, double breasted . . .'

Jump narrowed his eyes, 'Lady – you wanted a suit you

should've bought me one. I'm an actor, man, not a fuckin' fashion plate.'

And so their evening started. Jump, broody and discontented. Fontaine, ever so slightly embarrassed by her escort.

Several glasses of champagne later she couldn't have cared less. So what if he wore leather? He was six feet tall and had muscles in places other men didn't even have places. He would do very nicely to round off the evening with.

Jump was doing his best early Brando, and it was knocking everyone sideways. Boy, he could've laid every woman in the place – they all looked like they could do with a good seeing to. But he concentrated all of his energies on Fontaine. She was some lady.

They had met the previous week at a loft party in the village, and she had whisked him back to her apartment in a chauffeur-driven limo real quick. There, they had indulged in a four-hour sex marathon that had taxed even Jump's giant strength. Wow – some wild woman! And rich. And classy. And stylish. And he was sick of dumb twenty-year-olds anyway. And he wanted her to take him to London with her. He ached to go to Europe.

'Having fun?' Fontaine sneaked up behind him.

'Beats jackin' off.'

She smile, 'Oh my, you're *so* crude.'

'You like it.'

'Sometimes.'

'Always.' His hand slid around her backside.

She pushed it away, 'Not here.'

'You'd like it anywhere.'

'I knew there was something about you that I found irresistible – it's your perception and intelligence.'

He moved very close to her and grinned. 'Naw – it's my cock!'

☆

They made love for hours. It seemed like hours. It probably was hours.

Fontaine lay in bed, her head propped against the pillows, a cigarette in her hand. She was covered by a sheet in the semi-dark hotel room. Outside she could hear the occasional bleat of police sirens, and the usual New York street noises.

Jump was curled around in the foetal position at the foot of the bed. He was asleep, his muscled body twitching with occasional nervous spasms. He snored lightly.

Fontaine wished he had gone home. She wasn't too sure that she liked them staying the night. Why couldn't they just get dressed and go? In all honesty the only man she had ever enjoyed spending the night with was her ex-husband Benjamin, and that was strictly a non-sexual thing. Oh yes – they had made love on occasion – but Benjamin's stamina was low. To put it crudely, a two-minute erection was about all he could manage. So she had looked elsewhere for sex. And who could blame her? But Benjamin had been a friendly all-night companion – in spite of the fact that business calls came through from all over the world all night and every night – and *that* hadn't been too much fun. But still, she missed the basic companionship. The fact that at one time Benjamin had *cared* about her.

What did this muscled lump lying at the bottom of her bed care about? Certainly not her, that was for sure.

Oh maybe he liked her, was in awe of her, thought she could do him some good. But care? Forget it.

Most of the sexual athletes of this world were users. They bargained with their bodies. She should know – she had done it herself.

With a sigh Fontaine got up and went into the bathroom. She gazed at her reflection in the mirror. Her hair was a mess, and her make-up smudged. Good. Maybe Jump – what a positively *ridiculous* name – would take one look at her and leave. I must be getting old, she thought, with a wry smile, if all I have in mind is getting rid of him.

She ran the shower, and stood beneath the icy needles of water.

Jump stirred and woke. He reached up for Fontaine's leg, groped around, and realized that she wasn't there. He was annoyed with himself for falling asleep. After the sex should have come the talk. He was all ready to hurry back to his apartment, throw some clothes in a bag, and jet off to London with Fontaine. What would an extra ticket matter to her? Anyway he would give her plenty of value for money.

He could hear the sound of the shower. He leapt off the bed and padded into the bathroom.

Fontaine's body was silhouetted through the shower curtain. Jump didn't hesitate, he climbed right in with her. His entrance was spoiled by the fact that he hadn't realized it was a *cold* shower, and it took exactly two seconds for his powerful erection to become a shrivelled inch and a half!

Fontaine couldn't help laughing, but Jump was mortified.

By the time he recovered, Fontaine was briskly towelling herself dry, and brushed him away with a curt, 'Not now, I have to pack.'

Whiningly Jump seized his last chance. 'Hows about taking me with you?' he suggested. 'We could have ourselves a real good time.'

Fontaine had a fleeting vision of returning to London with a twenty-year-old, leather clad, dumb actor. *Not* exactly the image she wished to project.

'Jump,' she said kindly, 'one of the first things an actor should learn how to do is to make a good exit. You played your part beautifully, but, darling, this is the end of the New York run, and London is not exactly beckoning.'

Jump scowled. He didn't know what the hell she was talking about – but he recognized a no when he heard one.

5

'Cherry?' Nico's black eyes glared at Bernie, 'Why the *hell* did you bring her?'

They sat in the bar lounge together, and Bernie had never seen Nico so angry.

'I had no choice,' he explained weakly. 'She was there when you called, and she just sort of insisted.'

'There is always a choice in life,' Nico said bleakly, and he gazed off into space sipping his vodka.

Bernie coughed nervously. 'So?' he ventured, 'What's happening? Are we having fun?'

'We're having shit. How much money did you bring?'

Bernie patted his jacket pocket. 'Six thousand dollars – cash. Are we going to play it?'

Nico laughed mirthlessly. 'I have already played it my friend. I am indebted to this very fine Casino to the tune of five hundred and fifty thousand dollars. And that is not to mention the six hundred thousand of my own that I lost upfront.'

Bernie sniggered. 'What is this? Some kind of a joke . . .'

'No joke,' Nico snapped. 'The truth. Feel free to call me any kind of schmuck you like.'

They sat in uneasy silence for a few minutes, then Bernie said, 'Hey listen, Nico, since when did *you* become the last of the great gamblers? I mean I've seen you play enough times and you've never been into heavy stakes.'

Nico nodded. 'What can I tell you? I got greedy, and I guess when you get greedy your luck flies out of the window. Right, my friend?'

Bernie nodded. He had seen it happen before. When gambling fever hit, sometimes there was nothing you could do about it. It carried you along with a force that was breathtaking. Win or lose you couldn't stop.

'How are you going to pay them?' he asked.

'I can't,' Nico replied calmly.

'Jesus! Don't even kid around on the subject.'

'Who's kidding? I can't pay, it's as simple as that.'

'The Fonicettis would never have given you that kind of credit if they didn't know you were good for it.'

Nico nodded. 'I realize that now. But at the time I wasn't thinking straight, and nobody put a limit on my markers. I suppose they figured if I could lose six hundred grand of my own, then I didn't exactly have a cash flow problem. The six hundred was my house. My final stake. I'm broke, kid, busted out.'

The full enormity of Nico's dilemma was only just occurring to Bernie. To lose was bad enough. But not to be able to pay . . . Suicide . . . Pure undiluted suicide. Everybody knew what happened to bad debtors . . . Bernie personally knew a guy in LA who had owed the bookies seven thousand dollars. *Seven thousand measly dollars for crissakes.* He had been washed up on Malibu beach one morning, and the word had gone around that he was 'an example'. A lot of outstanding debts had got settled that week.

'You're in trouble,' Bernie said.

'An understatement,' Nico agreed.

'We'll figure something out,' Bernie replied, and as he spoke his mind was already checking out the limited possibilities.

☆

Cherry explored Nico's suite with childish delight. She even jumped up and down on the huge bed, and blushed when she thought of the fun they could have on *that* later.

Cherry had been in Los Angeles a little over a year, but already she had decided that the hustle and grind of being an actress was not for her. She had been a successful model in Texas when the call of Hollywood had brought her to a modest apartment on Fountain Avenue. Twenty-five auditions, two bit parts, and a commercial later, she had met Nico. Love had entered Cherry's life for the first time.

Sex had already entered it. First in high school with the football pro. Secondly with a blue jeans manufacturer. Thirdly with a Hollywood agent who promised her big things. She saw big things, but they weren't exactly what she had had in mind.

Nico was something else. He was everything she had always imagined a man should be. He was Nicky Ornstein, from *Funny Girl*. Rhett Butler, from *Gone With the Wind*, and Gatsby from *The Great Gatsby*.

Cherry always looked at life through the movies, things seemed more real that way.

Nico had swept her off her feet, from the moment they met at a party, to the moment he gave her his famous farewell speech.

At first she had cried and realized how right he was. Then she had thought, 'Why is he right? Why will I be happier without him?'

Then the thought had occured that without him she was miserable – so it stood to reason why they should be together.

Immediately she had rushed over to his house to tell him this exciting news, but he was not there, and Bernie had been kind enough to invite her to Las Vegas to find him.

She washed her hands, brushed her long golden hair, and sat and waited patiently. But after two hours she wondered if maybe she should go and look for them.

She checked her perfect appearance one final time, and set off to the elevator.

☆

Dino Fonicetti had often been told he was the absolute image of a young Tony Curtis. It was true. He was the best-looking goddamn guinea in the whole of goddamn Las Vegas, and as such he had the pick of the girls.

Not that appearance had that much to do with sexual success. His brother David had the misfortune to look like a mack truck, and he also scored with monotonous regularity.

Dino entered the elevator, and was stopped in his tracks by just about the most exquisite-looking female he had ever seen.

Of course it was the delectable and innocent-looking Cherry.

Dino said, 'Hello there.'

Cherry looked demurely at the floor.

Dino, master of the fast line racked his brains for something to say. He came up with, 'Are you staying at the hotel?'

Not a bad opening. Not particularly good.

Cherry looked at him with wide blue eyes, 'I'm just visiting,' she said primly.

Some answer. Everyone was just visiting in Las Vegas.

The elevator reached lobby level and stopped. They both stepped out. Cherry hesitated.

'Where are you going?' Dino asked.

'I'm meeting a friend.'

He decided that he couldn't just let this exquisite girl walk out of his life. He extended his hand, 'I'm Dino Fonicetti. My family owns this hotel and if there is anything at all I can do for you . . . anything . . .'

Her hand, as she gripped his, felt soft and small. He was in love. Pow! Just like that, he was getting a hard-on!

'I'm trying to locate Mr Nico Constantine. Do you know him?' Her voice was soft and small, almost as good as her hand!

Did he know Nico. Why, he was the very man he was looking for himself.

Did *she* know Nico? Shit!

☆

Nico and Bernie were still in a huddle discussing the possibilities, when Bernie said, 'I don't believe what I'm seeing. Dino Fonicetti is heading our way hand in hand with Cherry.'

Nico glanced around, and then stood as they approached the table.

Dino was indeed leading Cherry by the hand, determined not to let go. She went with him meekly, heads turning as she passed.

She looked at Nico, her eyes brimming over with the emotion of the moment. 'I had to come,' she murmured softly.

Nico's eyes flicked quickly between her and Dino.

'I met Mr Fonicetti in the elevator. He was kind enough to help me look for you,' Cherry said quickly.

'Nico!' Dino exclaimed warmly.

'Dino!' Nico's greeting was equally warm.

'And Bernie,' Dino added, 'why didn't you let me know you were coming?'

Bernie grinned, 'I didn't know I *was* until today.'

'Are you comfortable? Is everything all right?' Dino asked.

Nico grinned easily, 'Perfect.'

'Let me know if there's anything you need at all,' Dino said. 'By the way – how long will you be staying?'

The question was casual enough, but Nico felt he knew why it was asked. 'Long enough to recover some of my money,' he joked.

'Sure, sure,' Dino flashed his best Tony Curtis smile. 'We like everyone to leave here winners. Now tonight I want you all to be my guests for dinner.' He looked at Cherry. 'We'll catch Carlos Brent's late supper show. You'd like that, wouldn't you?'

She glanced at Nico. He nodded.

As a parting shot Dino turned to Bernie, 'Susanna's here,' he said. 'She looks great.' Then he strolled off.

'Who gives a shit,' Bernie muttered angrily.

Cherry asked, 'Who is Susanna?'

'Nobody important. Just my ex-wife.'

Nico was busily counting out some money. He handed Cherry two hundred dollars, 'Be a good girl, run along and play something. Bernie and I have things to discuss.'

'But, Nico. I want to talk to you. I have some very important things to say to you. I came all this way just to . . .'

'I didn't ask you to come,' he interrupted mildly.

Her eyes filled with tears. 'I thought you'd be pleased.'

'I am pleased, but right now I'm busy.'

Cherry pouted, 'I don't know how to gamble.' Nico pointed out Dino talking to one of the pit bosses.

'You friend will teach you. I have a feeling he'll be only too delighted to show you how it's done.' Cherry departed reluctantly, and Bernie and Nico exchanged glances. 'I think little Cherry is going to work in our favour,'

Bernie said. 'I haven't seen Dino so excited since he got laid by the whole of the Forum chorus line on two consecutive nights!'

'Right,' Nico agreed. 'Now let's go over the plan one more time.'

☆

Solicitously Dino offered Cherry more wine. She declined, holding a delicate hand over her glass to prevent him filling it. 'I never drink more than one glass,' she said solemnly.

'Never?' Dino chided.

'Never,' Cherry replied. 'Unless of course it's a wedding or a big event.'

'This *is* a big event,' Dino insisted, moving her hand and filling her glass to the brim. He felt extremely elated at the way things were turning out. Nico had practically handed over Cherry on a plate. The four of them had eaten together – then Nico had taken Dino to one side and explained that he had a late date, and that Cherry arriving in Vegas had been an embarrassment that he didn't need. Dino had assured him not to worry. He would be more than happy to take personal care of Cherry.

'She's a wonderful girl,' Nico had enthused. 'But no more than a sister to me now, and yet . . . well, I wouldn't want to hurt her feelings. I'll probably spend the night with my date . . .'

'I'll make sure Cherry never even finds out,' Dino said. If she spent the night with him how could she find out?

So after dinner Nico had made an excuse and left, and then Bernie had been set upon by his ex-wife Susanna, and gone off in a huddle with her, and now it was just Cherry and Dino.

Cherry was confused, but determined to help Nico out. He had asked her to keep Dino busy . . . 'Do anything, but be sure he is totally absorbed by you until at least noon tomorrow.' Nico had kissed her softly, 'It's important to me, and one day I'll explain it to you.'

Cherry sipped her wine slowly, 'Dino?' she questioned softly. 'Do you actually *live* in the hotel, or do you have a house?'

'I live right here, babe,' Dino said proudly. 'There are

five penthouses, and one of them is all mine. Best view of the strip you're ever likely to see – that's if you want to see it.'

'Ooh, I'd simply *love* to see it. Can I?'

Could she? Goddamn. Things were working out better than he had hoped.

Dino's full concentration was on Cherry. He forgot about everything else. Going to bed with this exquisite little doll was his prime concern. He quite forgot about the fact that he was supposed to quiz Nico about his markers and get his personal cheque to cover them. Five hundred thousand big ones was quite a debt by anyone's standards. But still . . . Getting to Cherry was enough to take anyone's mind off anything. And it wasn't like Nico was taking off anywhere . . . He was around. Dino would talk to him about it the following day.

☆

As soon as he made his excuses at the dinner and was able to get away, Nico headed straight for the Casino. His black eyes scanned the room searching for the lady who was to be his date.

Mrs Dean Costello scooped in another stack of hundred-dollar chips. God it was fun! It's a shame Mr Dean Costello hadn't dropped off a few years earlier. He had been so stingy with his massive fortune. Hadn't he realized that money was to have fun with?

Whoops – here came another number. Thirty-five. She had five chips on the centre and a cheval all round it.

'You're very lucky tonight, madame,' Nico said.

She turned to see who was speaking, and there, right behind her, stood that handsome sonofabitch from the baccarat table. She *knew* he had been after her.

'Yeah, I'm lucky,' she giggled, raking in her chips.

Nico watched her giant diamond ring catch the lights and sparkle invitingly. It had to be worth enough to get him out of trouble.

He wondered vaguely how much she weighed. Two hundred or three hundred pounds? Somewhere between the two.

He wondered how old she was. Fifty, maybe even sixty.

'You're a beautiful woman,' he muttered in her ear, 'and beautiful women shouldn't waste a night like tonight at the gaming tables.'

'Are you foreign?' she asked, flattered by his compliment but not surprised. Mrs Dean Costello thought that she was indeed beautiful. A few pounds overweight perhaps, and a little old for some tastes. But this guy was no chicken, and he knew a good-looking, *mature, sexual* woman when he saw one. He was no fool.

Busily she began to cash in her chips. Opportunities like this did not happen every day.

A half hour later they were in her room. When Nico wanted something he did not waste time.

'I don't usually invite strange men up to my room,' Mrs Costello giggled.

'I'm not strange,' Nico replied, opening up champagne and surreptitiously slipping two strong sleeping draughts into hers. 'What is so strange about wanting to be alone with a beautiful woman?'

Mrs Costello cackled with delight. This was the best one to come her way since the twenty-year-old black waiter in Detroit.

☆

Susanna had not been part of the plan – but what could Bernie do? She grabbed a hold of him, bossy as ever, and now she lectured him in an increasingly whiney voice about what a sonofabitch his lawyer was.

Bernie sat and nodded, hardly able to get a word in. He watched Dino and Cherry at a nearby table, and *that* all seemed to be going well.

Susanna tapped him sharply on the arm. 'I said, what are you doing here? Aren't you listening to me?'

'Sure,' he snapped back to attention and focused on Susanna. She had her mother's sharp features softened by a very good nose job.

'Well?' she glared at him.

'I didn't think I needed your permission.'

Susanna sneered, 'That's right, give me one of your smart-ass answers – that's all you know.'

Bernie stood up. He didn't need this crap. 'You'll have to excuse me, Susanna. I have a hot date with a black jack dealer. The cards are calling, and *that's* why I came here.'

'Gambling!' Susanna spat. 'And I have to fight you for every stinking cent of my alimony.'

He threw her a cold look. He was paying her fifteen hundred dollars a month, and she was insisting on more. It really was a joke. Carlos Brent was worth millions, and Susanna was his only child. Out of the corner of his eye he saw Cherry and Dino rise from their table.

'Got to go,' he said quickly.

'Bernie,' Susanna restrained him with a hand on his arm, her voice softening. 'Why don't we get together for a drink later? I really am sick of all the arguments.'

Oh, Christ! More complications! Susanna had that 'I wanna get laid' look about her.

Bernie managed an encouraging look. 'I'd like that. Where will you be?'

'I'm spending some time with daddy after the show, then I'll be in my room. Come for a drink.'

'Right. I'll see you later.' He made his escape just in time to check Cherry and Dino getting into the elevator. The kid had really come up trumps – one word from Nico and she was prepared to do anything to help.

Bernie hurried outside. He had his part to do as well.

They all wanted to help Nico.

6

New York's Kennedy airport was as busy as ever. The weather hadn't been too good, and a lot of people were sitting around and complaining, waiting for their flights to take off.

Fontaine Khaled arrived at the airport in her usual style. She swept in, followed by two porters organizing her luggage.

An airport official rushed over immediately.

Jump hovered in the background thinking about the day *he* would get treated in such a fashion.

'Mrs Khaled. So good to see you again,' said the official.

'Will you check me in?'

'Of course, of course. Would you like to wait in the lounge?'

Fontaine was irritated. 'There's not a delay is there?'

'Only slight.'

'Oh, Christ!'

The airport official signalled to a ground hostess. 'Escort Mrs Khaled to the lounge, please.'

'Lets go,' Fontaine beckoned Jump imperiously.

☆

Nico's flight from Los Angeles had arrived one hour previously. He was not delighted to discover that his ongoing flight to London was delayed. He sat in the VIP lounge sipping vodka and musing on the events that had led him to where he was. He felt strangely elated when he really should be scared shitless. Christ! Maybe he had been stagnating for the last ten years. What had seemed like a good time had certainly not sent the adrenaline coursing through his veins like it was now.

Bernie had been very helpful. It had been *his* suggestion that if Nico couldn't pay his markers he split.

'Don't stay around to explain,' Bernie had urged. 'Get the hell out – get the money – and don't let them find you 'til you have it.'

Good thinking. But Nico had no idea at all how he was going to get the money. Then it had come to him. An idea so out of character – and yet so obvious. He would steal the fat lady's ring – it must be worth at least as much as he had lost.

At first Bernie thought he was kidding. Then he saw that Nico was indeed serious, and his mind had started to work. Steal the ring. Get the hell out of Vegas without the Fonicettis knowing. Sell the ring. Pay off the markers – and then worry about compensating the fat lady – for Nico insisted that she must be paid back.

It was a bizarre plan, but they both decided it would work.

Dino's crush on Cherry took care of him watching Nico too closely, and she had entered into the spirit of the whole caper with great enthusiasm. Bernie hired a car – and once Nico had the ring, he took the car – drove back to Los Angeles – picked up some clothes – and headed straight for the airport.

Bernie had a friend – Hal – in London, who had connections, and would be able to get the right deal on the ring. London was far enough away for Nico to have time to operate. By the time the Fonicettis had even realized he had left Vegas, he would be back with the money.

Of course the plan had holes. The fat lady would start hollering the moment she woke from her drug-induced sleep. But Nico had given her a false name – and who would suspect him anyway? He had taken care to make sure that they had left the Casino separately, and their only connection was sitting next to each other at the baccarat table.

Bernie and Cherry would stay in Vegas, and make believe Nico was still there too.

Now Nico waited for his connecting flight, and fingered the ring lying loosely in his pocket. He was worried about customs. What if they stopped him and found it? Not a good thought.

A woman swept into the room. She was sophisticated, assured, and beautiful. Late thirties, very expensive, totally in control. Almost a female version of himself. He couldn't help smiling at the thought.

She was accompanied by a muscle-bound young man, who hung on to her every word. And her every word was very audible, as she spoke in a piercing voice that didn't give a damn about who might be listening.

'God! This is all so boring!' she said loudly. 'Why can't the bloody plane take off when it's supposed to?' She threw herself dramatically into a chair, shrugged off her sable coat, and crossed silken legs. 'Do order some champagne, darling.'

'Who *is* that?' Nico asked the girl serving drinks.

She shrugged. 'Mrs Khaled. Some Arab millionaire's wife. We have orders to look after her. She's been through here before and she's an absolute bitch.'

☆

Fontaine wanted Jump to leave. He was annoying her. He was so obvious it was pathetic. All those little hints about how he longed to go to Europe. How he would miss her desperately. How she was bound to miss him. And of course – hadn't their love-making been the most erotic and sensual experience ever.

'I don't think you should hang around here any longer,' Fontaine said abruptly, 'I think I might just try and have a sleep.'

'I can't leave you,' Jump replied anxiously. 'The flight might be cancelled. I don't mind staying.'

Of course he didn't mind staying. He was hoping she would change her mind and take him with her.

'No, darling, I insist. You're been here quite long enough.'

Jump stood his ground. 'I'll stay, Fontaine. You never know what might happen.'

Before she could reply a hostess appeared and announced that the flight was ready to board.

'About time,' Fontaine complained, standing up and allowing Jump to adjust her sable coat around her shoulders.

He moved as if to hold her in a passionate embrace. She

responded deftly, offering him an informal cheek to kiss. 'Not in public,' she murmured. 'I do have a certain reputation.'

'When will you call me?' he inquired anxiously, more concerned about a trip to London than her reputation.

'Soon enough,'she replied succinctly.

☆

Nico secured the seat next to Mrs Khaled for two reasons. One – who better than to unwittingly carry his diamond through British customs than an English woman who it would seem unlikely they would stop. Two – the flight ahead was long and boring, and while Mrs Khaled was slightly long in the tooth for his admittedly juvenile tastes, she at least looked like she could amuse him, and if his luck was in – perhaps play a passable game of backgammon.

He allowed Fontaine to settle into her window seat before taking his place.

She glanced at him, amazing kaleidoscope eyes summing him up.

He smiled, full Nico charm. 'Allow me to introduce myself, Nico Constantine.'

She raised a cynical eyebrow, he was attractive, much too old for her, and conversations she didn't need.

Nico was not to be brushed off, 'And you are . . . ?'

'Mrs Khaled,' she replied shortly. 'And I may as well warn you, that even though we are travelling companions for the next few hours, I am totally exhausted, and certainly not in the mood for polite conversations. You do understand, Mr er . . .'

'Constantine. And of course I understand. But perhaps I can offer you some champagne?'

'You can offer away. But let us not forget that they serve it free in first class.'

'I meant when we arrive in London. Perhaps dinner at Annabels?'

Fontaine frowned. How crass to have to cope with a man on the make when all she wanted to do was sleep. She glanced across the aisle at a thirtyish blonde in a striped mink coat, 'Try her,' she said coldly. 'I think you'll have more success.'

Nico followed her glance. 'Dyed hair, too much makeup, please credit me with some taste.'

Oh, God! What had she done to be stuck next to a man on the make. She turned and stared out of the window. Perhaps she should have brought Jump if only to protect her from bores on planes.

'Your seat belt.'

'What?'

'The sign is on.'

She fiddled for the seat belt, couldn't find one half of it. Nico realized it, and attempted to help her buckle up.

'I can manage, thank you,' she snapped.

Nico was perplexed. A woman who did not respond to his charm? Impossible. Unheard of. For ten years he had taken his pick of the best that Hollywood had to offer. Ripe juicy young beauties – at his beck and call day and night. Never a turn down. Always adoration. And now this . . . this English woman. So full of herself, waspish, and frankly a pain in the ass.

But still . . . If he wanted to plant the diamond on her he had to develop *some* line of communication.

The jumbo-jet was taxiing down the runway preparing for take-off.

'Are you nervous?' Nico asked.

Fontaine shot him a scornful look. 'Hardly. I have been flying since I was sixteen years old. God knows how many flights I have taken.' She shut her eyes. How many flights *had* she taken? Plenty. The first year of her marriage to Benjamin she had accompanied him everywhere. The perfect wife. Trips all over the world, boring business trips that had driven her mad, until at last she had begged off and only taken the interesting ones. Paris. Rome. Rio. New York. Acapulco. Marvellous shopping. Exciting friends. And then the lovers . . . Well, Benjamin had driven her to the lovers . . .

She felt the thrust as the big plane became airborne, but she kept her eyes tightly shut, didn't want to encourage her travelling companion to indulge in any more inane conversation. He *was* an attractive man. Not her type of course, much too ancient. Probably appeal to her friend Vanessa, who liked them a little worn.

☆

'You've been asleep for two hours,' Nico announced.

Fontaine opened her eyes slowly. She felt hot and creased, and the taste in her mouth was truly vile.

Nico handed her a glass of champagne. She sipped it gratefully.

'Do you play backgammon?' he asked.

'Oh God! So that's what you are.' She couldn't help smiling. 'A backgammon hustler! I should have known.'

Nico grinned. 'A backgammon player – yes. A backgammon hustler – no. Sorry to disappoint you.'

'But you look the part – my God, you're almost better dressed than I am!'

'That would be impossible.'

Suddenly they were talking and laughing. The stewardess served food and more champagne.

He wasn't so bad, Fontaine decided. Rather nice actually. And what a refreshing change to have a conversation with a man who was neither a fag nor a young stud. Idly she wondered if he had money. He was certainly dressed well enough – and the jewellery was expensive and in perfect taste.

'What business are you in?' she asked casually.

Nico smiled. 'Commodities.'

'That sounds like it could be anything.'

'It usually is, I don't like to be pinned down.'

'Hmm . . .' She fixed him with a quizzical look.

'And you? Where is Mr Khaled?'

'Benjamin Al Khaled no longer has the pleasure of being my husband. Ex is the word – but keep it to yourself – I get better service when the world doesn't know.'

Nico looked her over admiringly. I'm sure *you* would always get good service.'

'Thank you.'

Their eyes met and locked. There was that moment when nothing is said but everything is known.

Fontaine broke the look. God! Maybe it was the plane

trip, maybe she was overtired, but suddenly she felt incredibly horny.

'Excuse me,' she got up and moved past him to visit the toilet. She wanted to check out her appearance. She probably looked a mess.

Nico watched her go, and sniffed at the cloud of 'Opium' perfume she left behind. Lise Maria had always worn 'Jolie Madame'. It was the first time he had thought of his late wife in a long time. Lise Maria belonged in the past, wrapped in a beautiful memory he did not care to disturb. Why was he thinking of her now?

'Will you be watching the movie, Mr Constantine?' the stewardess inquired.

'What is it?'

'*The Fury*. Starring Kirk Douglas.'

'Sure – leave the earphones.'

'And Mrs Khaled?'

'Yes. Mrs Khaled will watch it too.'

Making decisions for her already! And thinking about how it would be in bed with a woman like that . . . It had been so long since he had had a woman. Plenty of girls – gorgeous sweet creatures who enjoyed his expert tuition . . . But to have a real woman again . . . A sophisticated sensual female . . .

Idly he wondered if she had money, what a plus *that* would be.

7

Polly Brand stirred in her sleep and reached out. Her arm encountered flesh, and she woke with a start. Then she remembered, grinned, and reached for her glasses. 'All the better to see you with my dear!' she giggled, as she trailed her fingers down her companion's back.

'Get off . . .' he mumbled, still half asleep.

'Oh come on,' Polly responded, full of enthusiasm. 'We've just got time to do it before we go to the airport.'

'Do what?'

'*It*, of course.' Her hand reached for his slumbering penis.

He moved away. 'I gotta sleep. Ten more minutes . . .'

'Ricky. I've got you a very good job, and I do expect you to be grateful – *very* grateful.'

'I'll be fucking grateful tonight. Right now I need sleep.'

Polly squirmed all over him. 'You'll be working tonight, Ricky Tick. Our Mrs Khaled will have you hard at it ferrying her around 'til all hours. The bitch never sleeps. She has to be seen – constantly – and your chauffeur duties will not be over 'til dawn. And that's when *I* like to sleep. So come on – let's fuck!'

Reluctantly Ricky allowed the energetic Polly to go to

work on him until he was in a ready state to do her bidding.

A six-minute thrash and it was over.

'Thanks a *lot*!' complained Polly.

'Morning is not my best time,' Ricky grumbled, reaching for his watch. '*Especially* not five-a-bleedin'-clock.'

'We have to be at the airport by seven. Mrs Khaled cannot be kept waiting, she'll throw a right mood if she is. Your new employer is *very* temperamental.'

'Can't wait. Are you sure this job isn't just one big drag?'

Polly giggled, 'You'll love it. You'll have a great time. If I know dear old Fontaine . . .'

'Yeah?'

Polly climbed out of bed still giggling. 'Just wait and see, you're in for a big surprise . . . If she likes you that is . . . And oh boy . . . I've got a feeling she'll like you.'

Fontaine Khaled and Ricky the chauffeur. The thought sent Polly off into gales of laughter.

Ricky followed her out of bed. 'Come on, share the joke.'

'You'll know soon enough.' Polly clicked a cassette into her tape deck and the sound of Rod Stewart filled the room. She proceeded to exercise to the sound of his voice – unconcernedly naked.

Ricky watched her for a minute, then he went into the bathroom. Funny little thing that one. She had chatted him up in his mini-cab two weeks earlier – and before he knew it he had quit his job to accept the position as Mrs Khaled's chauffeur. Well, driving a mini-cab was not for him. Too many bleedin' headaches. Now chauffeuring was another thing . . . If you had to drive around London day and night you may as well do it in a Roller.

Polly stretched to the ceiling, back to touch the floor. Twenty-four . . . twenty-five . . . Finished.

She couldn't be bothered to wash, a bad habit but no one had ever complained. She pulled on a fluffy angora sweater and tight jeans, knee-length boots, and pulled a comb through her short spiky hair. Make-up was lipgloss only. Her tinted glasses did the rest. Polly was not pretty – more unusual and certainly attractive. She was twenty-nine years old, and head of her own Public Relations outfit. Not bad for a girl who started out as a secretary at seventeen. Her firm represented Fontaine Khaled's discothèque 'Hobo', and Mrs Khaled called on her whenever she needed anything. Polly didn't mind. For each service she performed she added a little extra on the bill. Finding Ricky would be worth at least a couple of hundred.

He emerged from the bathroom clad in a pair of jockey shorts decorated with a garish picture of a rhinoceros and a slogan saying- 'I feel horny.'

'Christmas! Where did you get *those*?' Polly fell about laughing.

'My kid sister.' Ricky walked over to the mirror to admire himself. 'They look all right, don't they?'

'All right? They're a fucking scream!'

Ricky frowned. 'It's only a joke, no need to wet your panties.'

Polly tried to stop laughing. 'I didn't know guys actually *wore* things like that.'

Ricky's dignity was affronted. He pulled on his trousers quickly.

Polly leaned back and studied him through narrowed eyes. Great body. Thin, wiry, rock-hard thighs and stomach, and a nice tight ass. Sexy, sexy face, dirty blond hair, and when he was in the mood – a natural enthusiasm for screwing. Nice and normal. Not into grass or coke or tying you to the bed. Probably didn't even know what bondage was.

Fontaine Khaled . . . if she wanted to . . . would absolutely adore him.

☆

The interior of the plane was dark as the big jet winged its way towards England. The movie had finished, and now most of the passengers were asleep.

Fontaine wasn't.

Nico wasn't.

They were indulging in a necking session – teenage in its intensity.

Who could ever forget the excitement of one's first furtive gropings. The hands under the sweater, up the skirt. The lips, tongues, teeth. The eroticism of investigating a strange ear. The exquisite thrill of a clandestinely fondled nipple.

Fontaine felt as flushed as any fifteen-year-old. It was an amazing sensation. Nico, too, was filled with an unremembered excitement.

To touch but not to be really able to. To feel – but not properly.

Whoever said making love on a plane was easy was a fool. It was goddamn difficult. Especially when a stewardess flitted up and down the aisle every ten minutes.

So they contented themselves with the sticky fondlings of first experience. And it was erotic to say the least. It was also fun. And it was a long time since either of them could remember sex being fun.

'When I get you in London, Mrs Khaled, I want time, space, and the luxury of a bed,' Nico whispered. His fingers were on her thigh, travelling up, sneaking round the leg of her panties.

Fontaine's hand fiddled with the zipper on his trousers. She could feel his maleness through the silk of his under-shorts, and it was turning her on with a vengeance. 'Oh, yes, Mr Constantine, I think that could be arranged.'

The stewardess passed by, brisk and efficient. Could she see what was going on? They both remained stock still.

'I want to see your body,' Nico whispered. 'I know you have a very beautiful body.'

Fontaine traced the line of his mouth with her tongue, 'None of your bullshit lines please, Nico. None of your stock phrases. You don't have to play the perfect gentleman with me.'

She had him figured out pretty quickly. He liked that. 'So I want to fuck you,' he muttered. 'I want to fuck your beautiful body.' Christ! He hadn't felt free enough to talk to a woman like that since Lise Maria. Fontaine was right – he did open his mouth and out poured the perfect gentleman bullshit.

That's better,' Fontaine sighed. 'I want to feel you're talking to me, not doing your number.'

Their tongues played sensuous games. Then dawn and lightness started to filter through the windows, and it was time to stop playing and brush out clothes and adjust things.

The stewardess served them breakfast with a thin smile. She had seen what was going on – and frankly she was jealous. It wasn't like she hadn't seen it all before. But a man like Nico Constantine . . . Well – if he hadn't been stuck next to that Khaled bitch there might have been a chance for her.

Fontaine nibbled on some toast, sipped the awful coffee, and smiled at Nico. That was—'

He put a finger on her lips. 'Don't give me any of *your* bullshit lines.'

'But it was.'

'It was.'

They grinned at each other stupidly.

'I'd better go and get myself together,' Fontaine said at last. 'A little makeup job, and my hair needs mouth to mouth resuscitation!'

It wasn't until she had gone that Nico suddenly remembered the reason he had struck up an acquaintance in the first place. It didn't seem so important now. But he had the ring, and it was burning a hole in his pocket. If he asked Fontaine he was sure that she wouldn't mind taking it through customs for him. But why involve her? The best thing was to have her do it for him unknowingly.

She had taken her makeup case and left her purse. Easy. He glanced across the aisle. The dyed blonde in the striped mink coat was engrossed in conversation with a drunken writer who was en route to London to get married for the fifth time.

Nico opened the purse. Easy. A double zipped compartment into which he dropped the ring. Easy.

Fontaine returned, her hair pulled sleekly back, a subtle makeup emphasizing her perfect bones. She smiled at him. 'Have I got time for a cigarette before we come down to earth?'

☆

Ricky drove the large silver Rolls-Royce much too fast. Polly, enjoying an early morning joint, admonished him. 'Mrs K. sets the speed when you're driving her. Don't you forget it.'

'What's she like?' Ricky asked for the sixth time.

'Oh, you'll either like her or you'll hate her. She's a difficult lady. No in-betweens. Typical Gemini – only ever does what she wants to do – hears what she wants to hear.'

'Has she still got a lot of money?'

Polly shrugged. 'Who knows? "Hobo" ain't making it any more, but her old man was so loaded . . . Look out Ricky – you nearly hit that car. You're supposed to be a chauffeur, not a racing car driver. And don't forget – call me Miss Brand in front of her. Wouldn't do to let her know I'm screwing the hired help.'

☆

'Mrs Khaled. Welcome back to London.' Fontaine was greeted by an airport lackey paid to smooth the way for VIPs. He took her makeup case. 'This way, Mrs Khaled. Everything's taken care of. If we can just have your passport . . .'

She glanced around, looking for Nico. He stood at the back of a long line for foreign passports.

She waved, blew him a kiss, and swept right through British passport control.

Nico was impressed. Still married to her Arab billionaire or not she knew how to do things in style. What a stroke of genius planting the ring on her. No way would customs dare to stop her.

He thought about where he would take her for dinner. It was many years since he had been in London. But Annabels was always safe, then maybe a little gambling at the Clermont, and then bed. He anticipated a stimulating evening in every way.

☆

Fontaine feigned surprise at seeing Polly. 'So early, darling? You shouldn't have bothered.'

Polly knew that if she hadn't bothered, Fontaine would never have let her forget it.

They kissed, the usual insincere brushing of cheeks.

'You look gorgeous!' Polly exclaimed. 'Have you had a wonderful time?'

'Terrible actually. Didn't you hear about my robbery?'

They walked to the car where Ricky respectfully held the Rolls door open.

'No! How awful! What happened?'

'I was wiped out. They took everything, absolutely everything!'

'Your jewellery?'

'Not my jewellery. That – thank God – was in the bank.'

Ricky shut the door on them. So this was the famous

Mrs Khaled. Really something. She made Polly look like a bit of old rope.

☆

Nico stood in line patiently for twenty-five minutes. It was annoying, but a fact of life when entering a foreign country.

Naturally he was detained at customs. 'You have the look of an expensive smuggler!' Lise Maria had once told him. 'Don't ever change, I love that look!'

The customs official was polite but insistent. Every one of his Vuitton suitcases was opened up and searched. For one horrible moment Nico thought they might also search him, but luck was on his side, and he did not have to suffer the indignity of a body search.

At last he was free. He hoped that Fontaine had waited for him – she had mentioned something about her car and chauffeur meeting her. But she was nowhere to be seen. Long gone. He should have known she was not the sort of woman who would wait around.

Damn. It was annoying. He wanted to recover the ring as soon as possible. What if she discovered it? The idea of that was not a welcome one, but he would just bluff it out – tell her the truth – not about actually stealing the ring – just about her helping him through customs with it. And a good job too, considering he had been stopped.

Fontaine would probably be amused by the whole incident.

Still . . . it would be better if she didn't find the ring . . . which meant he had to see her as soon as possible.

He signalled a cab and directed the driver to the Lamont

Hotel. He had been warned that no one of any note stayed at the Dorchester since it had been bought by the Arabs. The Lamont was *the* place – quiet, very English, with an excellent restaurant comparable to the Connaught.

'Cor blimey, mate,' sneered the cabbie. 'Sure you got enough bleedin' suitcases?'

8

Cherry's first night with Dino was a mechanical affair. He took her to his penthouse apartment atop the Forum, showed her the view – which she admired. Fixed her an exotic liqueur – which she drank. Played her some sensual Barry White sounds – which she enjoyed. Then moved in for the kill.

'I don't make love on a first date,' Cherry said demurely, long brownish black eyelashes fluttering over huge blue eyes.

'What?' snapped Dino. He had a hard-on that was threatening to burst the zipper on his pants.

'I like you a lot,' Cherry continued in her sweet baby girl voice, 'and I admire you. But I can't make love to you, it's against my principles.'

'Principles!' exclaimed Dino. 'Forget your goddamn principles.'

'Don't get mad,' Cherry replied firmly. 'You have no right to expect me to do anything I don't want to.'

He looked her over, every gorgeous inch of her, and for the first time in his life realized he was getting a turndown. He couldn't offer her a better part in the show. She didn't want to be a cocktail waitress. If he proffered money she would throw it back in his face. But his father had taught him well – every woman has her price – and every smart man should be able to find out what that price is.

'What do you want?' Dino asked thickly.

Cherry shook her long blonde curls. 'Nothing,' she replied. 'But I like being with you, and if you want I'll stay the night with you – but I won't do anything, and you must promise not to force me.'

In all his many experiences with women this was a first. Dino was perplexed. He was also fascinated. He was also in love.

They spent the night together. They kissed. They caressed. She stripped down to a skimpy lace chemise that would give any red-blooded male a heart attack. He put on a bathrobe over a pair of restrictive jockey shorts.

He just did not believe what was going on. He fell asleep with a wrecking gut-ache, and woke at seven in the morning with the same nagging pain.

Cherry lay asleep beside him, yellow hair fanned out around her face, legs slightly apart, the chemise revealing just a wisp of lacy panties.

Enough was enough. Dino rolled on top of her, ripping her panties with one hand, and freeing himself with the other. He was inside her before she even awoke.

'Dino! You promised!' She was not as outraged as she might have been.

'That was last night,' he husked. 'Our first date. Now it's our second date and it's my turn to call the shots.'

Cherry didn't argue. She wrapped her long and beautiful legs around him and gave a little sigh. Nico was a marvellous man – but as he had pointed out – what kind of a future did she have with him?

Now Dino was a different matter . . .

☆

So far so good. Everything was going according to plan.

Bernie placed a stack of chips on red and watched black come up. Roulette. What a game. Why was he even bothering?

He glanced at his watch. Two o'clock in the morning. Nico should be well on his way.

He eyed one of the cocktail waitresses. It wasn't his imagination that she had been coming on to him all night.

He gestured for another scotch, and wondered if he should hit on her for a fast fuck. He decided against it. He had too much on his mind, and anyway sex drained his vital energies.

At that precise moment his name was paged, and he thought – Christ! The shit has hit.

He rushed to the phone. It was Susanna. She was drunk. Just what he needed in his life, a drunken ex-wife.

'I thought you were coming up for a drinkie,' giggle giggle, 'or something . . .?'

'Hey,' How should he play *this* one? He was in enough trouble with Susanna as it was. 'I called you earlier, guess you weren't back,' he explained.

'Daddy had a party,' she hiccoughed. 'Fifteen gofers, twenty hookers, and half the mob.'

The only time she put daddy down was when she was drunk. Then she saw him for the egotistical mean sonofabitch he really was.

Bernie played for time. 'Sounds like fun.'

'It wasn't. It was awful,' she paused, then in a sexy whine. 'Come on up Bernie, for old times' sake. We can just – talk.'

Oh shit! What did he have to lose?

Besides which, Susanna gave the best head in Hollywood. Or if there was anyone better *he'd* never found them.

☆

Cherry and Dino spent the morning in bed.

They talked. They investigated the possibilities of getting further involved. They would have stayed there all day if Dino's father hadn't called and demanded his presence.

'What I want you to do is go back to Nico's suite, collect your things, and tell him bye bye,' Dino told her.

At the mention of Nico's name Cherry felt a twinge of guilt. Surely if she was planning to stay with Dino her loyalties lay with him? Maybe she should tell him that Nico had already left . . . But then again she had promised Nico she would help . . . And of course she wouldn't want him to come to any harm.

Dino was dressing. White slacks, a black shirt, white sports jacket. Las Vegas casual.

Cherry sat up in bed, blonde hair tumbling around her shoulders. 'Dino,' she ventured shyly, 'have you ever been married?'

Dino grinned at himself admiringly in the mirror.

'Me? No, of course not.'

'Why of course not?'

'Well . . . gee . . . I don't know . . .' Why *hadn't* he ever got married? Never met anyone he would want to marry. He looked at Cherry lying in his bed. She was so . . . delectable . . . He wanted to eat her up. His grin widened, he would later.

She climbed out of bed innocently unaware of his scrutiny – or so he thought.

Now that was what he called a body. Streamlined and golden. Soft and firm.

She walked to the bathroom door, turned, and smiled sweetly. 'I'd *like* to get married,' she said softly. 'Wouldn't you?'

☆

Bernie did not escape Susanna's clutches until six in the morning. He staggered from her room bleary-eyed and exhausted. They had run through the whole book of emotions – plus some very wild sex.

He hurried back to Nico's suite, and collapsed on the bed.

He had blown checking with Nico on the phone, but hopefully, by this time, he was on a plane to Europe.

Now if the pretence of Nico still being in Vegas could only be kept up . . .

Bernie fell into a fully clothed sleep.

☆

As Bernie fell asleep Mrs Dean Costello woke up. She felt as if someone had hit her over the head with a hammer, and she was surprised to note that she was still fully dressed.

She struggled to recollect the events of the previous evening . . . But she just couldn't, her brain seemed to be all fogged up.

She vaguely remembered an extremely charming gentleman . . . Champagne . . . And hadn't she won a fair amount of money . . .?

Her winnings! She struggled to sit up, and switched on a light.

Her winnings were neatly stacked on the bedside table. Eighteen thousand dollars if her memory served her correctly. Propped beside them was a note—

'Madame. You are a charming and gracious lady – and I am sure you would help a gentleman out of trouble. I have borrowed your diamond ring – but the loan is temporary and you shall be repaid in full . . . I would appreciate your co-operation of not going to the police . . .'

Mrs Dean Costello started to laugh. Why that cocky son-of-a-bitch. The nerve. The goddamn bare-assed nerve.

9

The Chelsea house was looking a little tacky, Fontaine decided. It was part of the divorce settlement – Benjamin had kept their Belgravia mansion and she had been bought what she considered to be a rather unimpressive abode.

It was certainly not unimpressive. It was a five-bedroomed, three-receptioned-room elegant house with a large garden. However, it was not the Belgravia mansion with the indoor swimming-pool, sauna, private cinema, internal elevator, and landscaped roof-garden.

Fontaine had furnished her new house in a hurry before she had left for New York, and it did have style. The trouble was that nobody had been living there except Mrs Walters, her ancient and faithful housekeeper, and the rooms smelt musty and unused, and there was even the faint aroma of cat pee.

'Christ!' Fontaine exclaimed. 'Why the hell didn't someone air this place out? And why aren't there any fresh flowers?'

Polly shrugged. Fontaine's domestic arrangements really were not her affair.

'Mrs Walters!' Fontaine yelled.

The old woman came running out from the kitchen. 'Welcome home, Mrs Khaled—' she started to say.

Fontaine cut her short with a barrage of complaints.

Ricky came through the front door carrying some of the luggage.

Polly winked at him. He frowned.

'I never said she was easy to work for . . .' Polly murmured as he passed by.

☆

Nico checked into the Lamont Hotel and requested a suite. He was shown to a smallish suite overlooking the back. He handed the porter a five-pound note, and said, 'Stay here a minute.' Then he picked up the phone and asked to see the Manager immediately.

The Manager, Mr Graheme, was with him ten minutes later, a thin harassed man whose main concern at that moment in time was whether he could prevent the entire kitchen staff from walking out. Earlier in the day he had fired an assistant chef who had been caught stealing fillet steaks – handing them to an accomplice as he took out the garbage. This had resulted in a flat statement from the rest of the kitchen workers that either the thief stayed or they walked. What to do? Mr Graheme had still not decided.

'Yes, sir, what can I do for you?' he snapped at Nico, a little too harshly but he *was* under a strain.

Nico gestured at his surroundings, 'Nice,' he said warmly. 'Very comfortable.' Then he moved over to Mr Graheme and offered him a cigar, then he put his arm conspiratorially around his shoulders, 'Mr Graheme. I stay at your hotel for the first time. The place has been highly recommended to me by many of my friends in

Beverly Hills. But really . . . a suite like this for a man like me . . . Perhaps I should try the Connaught . . .'

Fifteen minutes later Nico was ensconced in the best suite in the hotel.

Mr Graheme knew a big spender when he saw one.

☆

Once rid of Polly, Fontaine couldn't wait to get on the phone to Vanessa Grant, her very best friend in London.

'I'm back,' she announced dramatically. 'Exhausted and destroyed. I can't wait to see you. How about dinner tonight?'

Vanessa hesitated, she and her husband Leonard already had dinner plans, but once Fontaine wanted something it really didn't do to argue.

'I think that will be fine,' she said.

'Fine!' Fontaine snorted. 'Bloody enthusiastic welcome that is!'

'We weren't expecting you until next week . . .'

'I know, I know. I had to change my plans because of my *robbery*.'

'What robbery?'

'Darling – haven't you heard? It's all over the papers in New York.'

They chatted some more, arranging where and when to meet, then casually Fontaine asked, 'By the way, do you and Leonard know a man called Nico Constantine? An Americanized Greek. Lives in Beverly Hills, I think.'

'No, I don't think that name rings any bells. Who is he? Another of your juvenile delinquents?'

'Hardly juvenile, rather more mature.'

Vanessa laughed. 'Dcesn't sound like you at all. Is he rich?'

'I don't really know . . . Maybe.'

'Are you bringing him tonight?'

'Certainly not. I have a rather divine Italian Count who is flying in especially to see me.'

Vanessa sighed, she had been married for too many years and had too many children. 'Sometimes I envy you . . .'

'I know,' replied Fontaine crisply. 'If you're a good girl I'll throw him your way when I'm finished with him. He's twenty-six years old and horny as a rutting dog!'

☆

It occured to Nico that he had no idea how to get in touch with Fontaine. He had been so sure that she would wait for him at the airport that he had not even bothered to find out her phone number. Stupid really. But usually women waited . . . And after their undeniably erotic encounter on the plane he had felt sure that Fontaine would not go rushing off. Well, hardly rushing . . . Between passport control and customs it had taken him an hour to emerge. But still . . . She could at least have left a message.

He called the reception desk, told the porter her name, and asked him to find out her phone number and address immediately.

Half an hour later the porter gave him Benjamin Al Khaled's London office number, and a frosty secretary there said she could not possibly reveal the previous Mrs

Khaled's phone number or address, and if he wished to contact her he should write in and his communication would be forwarded on.

Nico turned on his telephone charm – not as potent as the real thing – but effective enough to get him the number with a little gentle persuasion.

He phoned Fontaine immediately. A housekeeper answered his call and said that Mrs Khaled was resting and could not be disturbed.

He left his name and number and a message for her to call him back. Then he contacted the hotel florist and sent her three dozen red roses with a card saying – 'The flight was memorable – when do we come in for landing? Nico.'

Next he phoned Hal – Bernie's London friend, whom he had never met – but who apparently knew everyone and everything – and who would be able to take excellent care of the ring situation – once he had it back of course.

They arranged to meet in the bar later.

Nico then called for the valet. Time to get his personal grooming in order. It would never do to look anything but perfect.

☆

Fontaine slept all day. At seven o'clock Mrs Walters woke her, and she got up and started her numerous preparations for the evening's activities.

'A Mr Constantine phoned,' Mrs Walters informed her. 'Also Count Paulo Rispollo. They would both like you to phone them back.' Mrs Walters busied herself with running Fontaine's bath. She had worked for her for over ten years and felt she understood her – although Fontaine was extremely difficult to work for, what with her sudden screaming fits and unreasonable demands.

'Call the Count back, tell him to collect me at nine o'clock.' Fontaine handed Mrs Walters a number. 'And if Mr Constantine phones again you can say I'm out.'

They both sent flowers,' Mrs Walters continued. 'Three dozen roses from Mr Constantine. A bowl of orchids from Count Rispollo. I told the new chauffeur to be back at eight sharp, shall I send him to pick the Count up?'

'I suppose so,' Fontaine stripped off her thin silk dressing gown and stretched. 'I don't think for one moment he has his own.'

Mrs Walters scurried off, and Fontaine climbed into a deliriously hot bath.

Count Paulo Rispollo. Young. Good-looking. Unfortunately didn't have a pot to piss in. But he adored her. Had met her in New York and declared undying love. Probably bi-sexual, but very passable in bed – and that's where it all mattered – wasn't it? Besides, it was so good for her image ... A young good-looking escort ... especially a titled one.

She thought briefly of Nico Constantine, then put him quickly from her mind. Trouble. She sensed it. And anyway – since when did she date men older than herself? What a positively boring idea. Who needed real conversations? All she needed was a fine young body – no complications – just sex. And if sometimes she had to pick up the bills ... well, that was life, wasn't it?

☆

Nico was irritated when Fontaine failed to return his call by the time he met with Hal. He was more than irritated, he needed to recover the ring urgently.

Hal turned out to be an amiable fortyish American promoter operating out of London. Attractive, if you liked the Dean Martin gone-to-seed type. Constantly stoned, and well dressed. His speciality was hustling elderly widow ladies.

He greeted Nico warmly, asked after Bernie, and mumbled, 'Where's the item? I have a good set up waiting to accept. I'm working on a split percentage – five per cent from you – five from them – does that suit you?'

'Sure, but I have a problem,' Nico explained. 'I met a woman on the plane. I thought it would be safer for her to bring it in. I don't have it back yet.'

Hal made a face, 'I was given to understand time was of the essence.'

'It is, it is. The woman . . . I'm trying to reach her. Her name is Fontaine Khaled.'

Hal let out a whistle. 'The ice queen herself! Is she back?'

'Do you know her?'

Hal laughed. 'Sure I know her. She owns "Hobo". My good friend Tony Blake used to run it for her – along with a few more personal services. He's living in LA now trying to recover from the experience! What the hell was she doing with *you*? You're a little over her age limit.'

'What the hell was *I* doing with *her*? Nico retorted quickly. 'She's a little over mine.'

'Does she know about the ring?' Hal asked.

'No. I hid it in her purse. I've been trying to contact her.'

'Don't worry. We'll see her tonight. The first place Mrs Khaled will go is "Hobo". We'll be there to greet her.'

☆

'What you need is another Tony,' Vanessa whispered. 'Franco just doesn't have it where it counts.'

Fontaine glanced around the half-empty restaurant at 'Hobo'. She didn't even know any of the people who were there – a dreary-looking bunch of bores.

'Do *you* know who any of these people are?' she asked Vanessa.

'Absolutely not,' Vanessa replied. 'It seems anyone can get in nowadays. Now when Tony was here . . .'

'For Christ's sake do shut up about Tony. I know you had the hots for him, but he's long gone. He got a little too big for his . . . boots.'

'Or something!' giggled Vanessa.

'Quite.' agreed Fontaine. She glanced around the restaurant again. It was a bore – but it was quite obviously true, 'Hobo' was no longer *the* place to be seen. Franco had let things run to rack and ruin.

Count Paulo seemed to be enjoying every minute. His boyish face glowed with the thrill of being out with the glorious Fontaine Khaled. He watched her admiringly. Leonard, Vanessa's husband, tried to indulge him in a business dialogue, but Paulo was more interested in gazing at his date.

Fontaine tapped impatient scarlet fingernails on the

table. 'Why don't we move on,' she suggested. 'Where *is* everyone going now?'

'There's a divine new club called "Dickies",' Vanessa enthused. 'Gay, of course – well, more mixed really. The waiters wear satin shorts and roller skates and they serve the most decadent drinks, they make you drunk for a week!'

'Let's go,' said Fontaine. 'I think I should see where the real action is.'

She rose from the table and swept out of the restaurant.

Franco snapped to attention. 'Mrs Khaled, you 'ees leaving so early. Something the matter?'

'Yes, Franco,' her voice was cold. 'You, as it happens. You're fired.'

☆

Hal produced two beautiful girls. A black croupier on a two-week vacation, and a streaked blonde who was into meditation. Nico got the blonde, although he insisted to Hal he didn't want a date.

'It'll look better,' Hal explained. 'Trust me, I know Fontaine. Besides, tonight is my night off. Once a week I treat myself to a broad under sixty.'

'So have two,' Nico suggested. 'I don't want one.'

They arrived at 'Hobo' ten minutes after Fontaine had left.

'Mrs Khaled around?' Hal asked Franco.

'She come, she go.' Franco replied, then he burst into a stream of Italian abuse about his soon-to-be-former employer.

'Nobody ever called Fontaine a pussycat,' Hal agreed.

'A beetch!' Franco shrieked. 'I work my ass to the bone – and like that – poof – she throw me out.'

'Yeah,' said Hal. 'Like Tony. Remember Tony? You took his job.'

Franco glared.

'Come on,' Hal said to Nico. 'Knowing our Fontaine, she's checking out the competition.'

☆

Fontaine was indeed checking out the competition, and she could see immediately why 'Dickies' had taken over. The disco music was great, the waiters outrageous, and the whole ambience reminded her of 'Hobo' when it had first opened.

Her kaleidoscope eyes surveyed the scene. Yes – All the same old faces. Every *one* of the 'Hobo' regulars.

'Fun, isn't it?' Vanessa enthused.

'Hmmm . . . Not bad.' Fontaine turned to Count Paulo, 'Let's dance.'

The floor was crowded – unlike the barren expanse at 'Hobo'. As Fontaine moved her body expertly in time to the Bee Gees, her mind was racing. What 'Hobo' needed was a revamp. New lighting. A change of menu. Definitely a different disc jockey. And a manager with the charisma Tony had possessed.

The music changed to a horny Isaac Hayes singing 'Just the way you are.'

Count Paulo pulled her close. Funny, but she didn't fancy him one little bit. He just seemed . . . boring.

'Fontaine, gorgeous! When did you get back?' Suddenly

she was the centre of attention – so-called friends greeting her on all sides.

She smiled and nodded and enjoyed the scrutiny. She was no fool. She knew what they were all thinking – Poor old Fontaine – no more millionaire husband – no more successful discothèque. What was she going to do?

Well, she bloody well wasn't going to do what they all wanted – fade away defeated. She was back with a vengeance, and they'd better all believe it.

'Hello darlin' what you doin' here? "Hobo" not the same since you threw Tony out?'

She turned to confront the owner of the raucous cockney accent. It was Sammy, a small wiry-haired dress manufacturer who only went out with girls under the age of sixteen.

Fontaine smiled coldly. 'I'll find another Tony. He was never an original.'

'Oh, yeah?' Sammy winked knowingly. 'What you need is a guy like me to run the place for you. I'd soon get it all back together – 'ave 'em raving in the aisles in no time. Want to give me a try?'

Fontaine looked him over with a mixture of amusement and contempt. 'You?' the one word said it all.

'All right, all right, I know when I'm not appreciated,' Sammy backed off.

Count Paulo rubbed her thighs. 'Who was that?' he asked possessively.

'Do you have to hold me so tight?' Her voice was ice. 'You're creasing my dress.'

☆

Nico noticed Fontaine immediately. Well, she could hardly be missed. She certainly was striking.

He watched her on the dance floor clutched in the arms of some young stud. She obviously had a predilection for young studs – just as he had for fresh-faced young beauties.

'Told you she'd be here,' Hal announced triumphantly.

'Can we dance, Nico?' The black croupier was pulling on his jacket sleeve. 'Hal won't mind – he doesn't dance.'

Nico gently removed her tugging hand and adjusted his sleeve. 'Not right now, dear.'

Hal spotted his friend Sammy, and moved over to join him and his teenage companion.

After introductions Hal explained to Sammy that Nico wanted to get together with Fontaine.

Sammy laughed. 'Are you kidding? No chance, her highness wouldn't sniff in your direction!'

'Oh, yes?' Nico headed confidently towards the dance floor. 'Just watch her sniff!'

10

In Las Vegas, Bernie Darrell began to realize that protecting Nico was not exactly going to do him any good. Okay – so he was on fairly friendly terms with Dino Fonicetti – and he knew the father and the brother to nod to. But they were hard people . . . They had their reputation to consider . . . And when the fact that Nico had skipped town owing five hundred and fifty thousand grand was revealed . . . And then it came out that he, Bernie, had helped in the deception . . . Well . . .

By Tuesday evening he was apprehensive. And when Cherry baby came knocking at the door to pick up her things he was even more so.

'I shall have to tell Dino that Nico has left,' Cherry announced. 'I refuse to lie.'

Bernie was startled. 'What the hell are you talking about?' he snapped. '*We're* helping Nico – remember?'

'I have a certain loyalty to Dino,' Cherry replied primly.

'Loyalty? To Dino?' Bernie was amazed. 'What the *fuck* are you talking about?'

Cherry was oblivious to his anger as she packed up the few things she had brought with her. 'Of course, I won't mention that Nico left last night, I'll just say he's gone—'

Bernie grabbed her wrist roughly. 'You'll do no such fucking thing!'

'You're hurting me,' Cherry's blue eyes filled with tears. 'I'll tell Dino.'

Bernie released her. 'I don't believe this! I just don't believe it!' He mimicked her voice – '"I'll tell Dino . . ." What is this – love's young dream all of a sudden? A one-night screw and the blonde and the hood see stars?'

Cherry raised her voice for the first time since Bernie had known her. 'It is possible, you know, for two people to fall in love. Dino is a warm and kind human being . . .'

'Holy shit!'

'We're going to get married if you must know.'

'I need a drink,' Bernie fixed himself a large scotch. His mind was racing. This was a beautiful situation. It could only happen to him. One moment the dumb cunt was trailing Nico to Las Vegas determined to sort out their future together. The next – true love with a mafioso one-night stand. Unbelievable!

He tried to soften his voice. 'Hey, Cherry – I'm really pleased for you and Dino, really I am. But if you tell him Nico has split, we're all in trouble – you included.'

'Not me,' Cherry protested indignantly.

'Yes – you, baby. How do you think your future bride-groom is going to feel when I tell him last night was a set-up?'

'What do you mean?'

'You spent the night with Dino so that Nico could get out of town. Right?'

'I suppose so . . .'

'Don't suppose. It's a fact of life. Now if Dino finds that

out he is not going to be exactly thrilled.' Bernie took a deep breath. 'So listen carefully. You know nothing. Nico was here today when you picked up your things. You told him goodbye – that's all you know. And as far as you're concerned he's still here.'

'But I still think—'

'Will you listen to me sweetheart. Listen and learn. If your future plans include being Mrs Fonicetti, play it my way. You tell Dino the truth, and who knows how he'll react. Personally I wouldn't want to risk it.'

Cherry frowned. Bernie did have a point. 'Well, all right,' she said hesitantly. 'But when will Dino find out that Nico has gone?'

Bernie poured himself another scotch. 'By the time he finds out, Nico will be back – so don't you worry your pretty little head about it.'

Cherry nodded. 'OK Bernie, if you say so.'

So far so good. But could she be trusted? She was such a fucking idiot. Bernie sighed. How the hell had he ever got involved in this whole caper? Here he was – stuck in Las Vegas. What about his business? He had meetings to attend, and it would be at least a couple of days before Nico returned. That was if all went according to plan.

Cherry was packed up and ready to go. She smiled sweetly at him and stuck out a small delicate hand.

'Goodbye Bernie, and thank you for everything.'

Christ! She sounded like she'd taken a course in good manners!

'Yeah . . . well . . . I won't be leaving yet, so I guess we'll be seeing each other around. Now don't forget what I told you. Be a smart girl and you'll go far.'

She departed.

Bernie made a few mental calculations. Nico should be arriving in London about now. Hal was alerted to the situation. If all went smoothly the ring would be sold and the money in Nico's pocket within twenty-four hours. He would get on a plane immediately and be back in the suite before anyone realized he was gone. Pay off his markers. Back to LA. Mission accomplished. No broken bones.

It sounded easy.

Bernie wished the whole goddamn caper was over and done with.

11

'Mrs Khaled,' Nico cut in on the dance floor, subtly elbowing Count Paulo aside. 'What a pleasure to see you again so soon.'

'What do you think you are doing!' Count Paulo exploded. 'You cannot—'

'It's all right, Paulo,' Fontaine waved him aside. 'Run along and sit down, I'll join you in a minute.'

The Count glared, then reluctantly departed.

Nico took her in his arms, even though the beat was strident disco.

'Nice-looking boy,' Nico remarked. 'Similar to the one with you at Kennedy airport.'

'Yes. I like them full of energy.'

Nico raised an eyebrow.

Fontaine laughed.

'Did you get my flowers?' he asked.

'Very nice. How did you find my address?'

'If I want something I usually manage to get it.'

'Oh, really? We're so alike.'

'Thank you for waiting at the airport.'

'I'm hardly a taxi service.'

'I thought we had a date.'

'A date? How delightfully old world of you.'

'Has anybody ever told you that you're a bitch?'

'Frequently.'

Nico pulled her in very close indeed. Count Paulo, skulking at the edge of the dance floor, glared.

'Well, Mrs Khaled,' Nico said softly, 'are we going to finish what we started on the aeroplane?'

Fontaine responded to his maleness. 'Why not, Mr Constantine. Why not indeed?'

☆

'Bleedin' hell!' Sammy exclaimed, as they all watched Nico and Fontaine exit. ''E's only done it! What's 'e got? Mink-lined balls!'

'Oh, Sammy, you are awful!' his teenage girlfriend squealed.

'The guy has a lot of charm,' Hal stated. 'Not to mention the best tailor I've ever seen.'

'Charm schmarm – all Fontaine wants to know about is the size of the bank balance or the cock!'

'Honestly Sammy!'

'It's all right darlin' – you'll be OK on both counts!'

☆

'I do believe she's leaving,' Vanessa whispered to Leonard.

'I think you're right,' he replied.

'Absolutely charming – you'd think she'd have the manners to say goodnight.'

'Nobody ever accused Fontaine of having any manners. Who is that man anyway?'

Vanessa peered at the couple swiftly leaving the dance floor.

'I don't know, he doesn't look her style at all – slightly too mature . . . but rather attractive.'

'Rich, I suppose,' said Leonard brusquely.

'Yes, I suppose,' Vanessa agreed.

'Oh, God!' Leonard exclaimed, 'Don't tell me we're stuck with her Italian juvenile.'

'Looks like we are.' Vanessa watched a surly Count Paulo approach. Oh yes. There was certainly something to be said for the young ones . . .

Maybe if Fontaine had finished with him . . .

Vanessa wasn't proud. She had accepted seconds from her friend before.

☆

Ricky tried to concentrate on his driving, but it wasn't easy. God Almighty – you would think he had a couple of teenage ravers in the back. He attempted to keep his eye on what was happening in the rear-view mirror. Naturally Mrs Khaled had pressed the button which sent the glass partition up cutting him off from their sounds.

He drove the Rolls-Royce slower than usual, until Fontaine lowered the glass partition an inch and snapped, 'Do hurry up, Ricky.'

Bitch!

He wondered if he was free after he dropped her at her house. He was feeling extremely randy, and wondered if Polly would be up . . . Better than sleeping the night in that pisshole of a room he had rented.

The Rolls glided up to Fontaine's house. Ricky jumped out and opened the car door for them. He gazed disinterestedly off into space.

'Will you be needing me again tonight, Mrs Khaled?' he ventured.

'No, Ricky,' her voice was light and full of excitement. 'Tonight I will not be needing you.'

'What time tomorrow, Mrs Khaled?'

'Ten o'clock – I'd like you here every morning at ten o'clock.'

'Yes, Mrs Khaled.'

He waited until they turned to walk in the house, then he glanced at his watch. It was already two in the morning. Some job. It was a good thing the wages were right.

He wondered what had happened to the Italian ice cream. Must have got himself dumped . . .

Ricky couldn't help smiling. He liked a woman who behaved like a man.

☆

It was an erotic experience.

It was clothes off on the stairs.

It was hot tongues and warm bodies.

It was touch – feel – smell.

Fontaine felt herself out of control for once. Here was a man she didn't have to tell what she wanted. He knew everything. He was very . . . accomplished.

'You're like a dancer,' he breathed in her ear. 'You make love like a dancer who has been in training.'

'Hmmm . . . And you . . . you're like a stallion . . .'

He laughed. 'The Greek Stallion. It sounds like a bad movie! When I was twenty I was a stallion – now I *know* what I'm doing.'

'You certainly do!'

They made love endlessly – or so it seemed to both of them. And they were comfortable together – there was none of the awkwardness that sometimes happens the first time two people are in bed together.

The added bonus was that they could talk, not about anything special, just conversation.

Fontaine never had conversations with her transient studs – sometimes verbal skirmishes, but never conversations.

The same applied to Nico and his fresh-faced beauties. How boring and bland they all seemed once the initial thrill of a new body was over.

The thing that turned him on about Fontaine more than anything was her mind. She might be one tough lady – but she had wit and perception, and he wanted to dig deeper and find out more about the woman beneath the sophisticated veneer.

'I want to know all about you,' he said softly, 'who – why – how. From the beginning.'

Fontaine rolled over in bed. She felt delightfully satisfied. '*You're* the man of mystery. I meet you on a plane – the next minute we're in bed. But all I know about you is your name. You could be—'

'What?' He pinned her arms to the bed playfully. 'A mass murderer? A maniac?' He kissed her hard and released her. 'And don't tell me Mrs Khaled hasn't gone to bed with a man she met on a plane before.'

'Well . . . once or twice.'

'Oh, yes, once or twice I bet.' He smiled. 'How many men *have* you had?'

Fontaine stretched and got out of bed, 'Let's put it this way, Nico – a meal a day means you never go hungry.'

'Come back here, I want my dessert!'

'I'm going to take a shower, I need reviving. Why don't you go downstairs and bring up some Grand Marnier, I'll show you a delicious new way to drink it.' She went in the bathroom and closed the door.

Nico lay back still smiling. He felt fantastically relaxed. Then he remembered the ring. Wasn't that the reason he was here? Well, originally . . .

He could hear water running in the bathroom. He got off the bed and looked around the room for the purse Fontaine had carried on the plane. He couldn't see it around, but the mirrored door of a large walk-in closet stood invitingly open. He peered inside. Racks and racks of shoes stacked in neat rows. Shelves for sweaters, shirts, T-shirts, scarves, gloves. Belts and beads hanging in rows. Underclothes in perspex drawers. And handbags. All on a bottom shelf. About twenty-five of them.

He looked through them quickly, searching for the Gucci stripe. There were five with Gucci stripes, but none were the right one.

He swore softly under his breath, then suddenly saw the one he was looking for. It was hanging on the back of the door.

He grabbed it quickly, unzipped the side compartment, and there, nestled at the bottom, was his ring.

Fontaine appeared at the wrong moment, a pink towel wrapped around her sarong style. Her voice was icy, 'What exactly do you think you are doing?'

Nico jumped. He felt like a schoolboy caught with his hand inside the cookie jar. He wished he had put his pants on at least. There is nothing more daunting for a man than to be caught in an awkward situation with a limp dick hanging down.

'Well?' Fontaine could make one word a meal.

Nico smiled. Charm. His smile had got him through many tricky situations. 'You're never going to believe this.'

'Try me.' Her glacial expression did not crack.

'Well . . .' he tried to edge past her back into the bedroom.

She blocked his way.

'It's a long story,' he said quickly. 'I'm sure it will amuse you. Let me put some clothes on . . .'

Patiently, calmly, Fontaine interrupted him. 'Just tell me what you were doing in my bag – and just show me what you have in your hand. Now, Nico, right now. I don't want to hear any amusing stories, I'm not really in the mood for a good laugh.'

Nico shrugged, 'I can assure you I'm not taking anything of yours.'

'I can assure you of that too.'

'I had this ring . . . I thought maybe I would have problems with customs . . .'

He opened his hand and showed her the diamond.

She looked at it briefly, then at him.

'I was going to ask you if you would mind bringing it through for me . . . but I didn't know you that well . . . Of course, I was going to tell you—'

'You bastard. You son-of-a-bitch nasty little hustler,' her words struck icily through his. 'You *used* me – on the plane, this evening. How *dare* you!'

'I only—'

She held up an imperious hand. 'I don't want to hear. I just want you out – of my house, my life.'

'But Fontaine . . .'

She wasn't listening. She was in the bedroom gathering his clothes together, and when he emerged from the closet she threw them at him. 'Out!' she snapped. 'Before I have you thrown out.'

'I think we should talk about it.'

'Why? What more do you want from me? You've fucked me every way you can – and I might add that the screwing I got in bed wasn't half as good as the screwing I *really* got from you.'

She walked into her bathroom and slammed the door.

Quickly Nico got dressed. There was no point in staying around to argue. After all – he had what he had come for.

12

'What?' Joseph Fonicetti regarded his youngest son through narrowed eyes. 'What the fuck did I just hear you say?'

Dino shuffled his feet uneasily. How come everywhere he was a king – and in front of his father – zero – nothing – a goddamned kid again.

'I . . . I . . . er . . . well . . . I'm gonna get married.'

Joseph threw him a long unnerving stare. 'Just like that. Out of the blue you've found yourself a girl fit to be your wife. In *Las Vegas* you've found a girl to take the Fonicetti name. What is this beauty? A showgirl? A cocktail waitress? A *hooker*?' Joseph spat with disgust into a handy ashtray.

'She's a very lovely girl,' Dino said quickly. 'Not from Las Vegas.'

'None of them are *from* here – they only come here to develop their cunts and their bankrolls!'

'She's a nice girl,' Dino said defensively. 'You'll love her.'

Joseph shut his eyes and mulled over the fact that Dino was a good-looking boy, but when it came to women he was dense. Now David, his elder son, was smart. He had a wife, a plain Italian girl who would never give him a moment's trouble, and he fucked around with Las Vegas gash on his terms only.

'When did you meet this girl?' Joseph asked. 'A month? Two months ago? How come I've never heard you mention her before?'

'Well, Cherry only got here this week . . . You know how it is . . . this is the girl I want to marry. It happened just like that.'

Yes. Joseph knew how it was. Some smart broad had hooked her little finger round Dino's cock and thought she was going to get lucky. Well, she could think again. When Joseph was ready for Dino to get married – *he personally* would arrange it. A selection of Italian virgins would be shipped in – just as they had been for David – and Dino could take his choice.

'So . . . this Cherry. Who did she come here with?'

Dino answered quickly. He wanted to lie, but his father would find out the truth anyway. 'She came here with Bernie Darrell, they're just friends.'

'Sure. Bernie Darrell brought a girl all the way to Vegas and they're just friends. I believe that. Who wouldn't?'

'She came to see Nico Constantine, then she met me. Neither of us expected this . . . it just happened.'

'And what did Nico do? Kiss you both and wish you luck?'

'She and Nico . . . It was over anyway.'

Joseph nodded. 'Of course, she wasn't influenced by the fact that Nico was losing his ass at the tables. By the way – have you made arrangements with him about paying?'

'I will, I will.'

'Sure – leave it go while you make wedding arrangements. Who cares about five hundred and fifty thousand dollars.'

'Nico's good for the money.'

'He'd better be.'

'He is. I'll deal with it today.' Dino coughed nervously. 'Now, about Cherry. When can I bring her to meet you?'

Jospeh nodded thoughtfully, he had an idea. 'Tonight,' he said, 'we'll have dinner. The whole family. We'll discuss your wedding plans.'

Dino was relieved. It seemed his father was accepting Cherry without too much of a fight. Well – he must have known it was no use fighting – after all – he, Dino, was not exactly David who could be forced into a dull marriage with a placid Italian lump.

Dino smiled. They would all love Cherry. From the moment Joseph met her it would be smooth sailing.

☆

'We have an invitation,' Susanna said, sitting down and joining Bernie in the coffee shop.

'We do?' He was halfway through a prune danish – wondering if it would solve his bowel problem.

'Yup.' Susanna studied the menu. 'Daddy wants us to have dinner with him and the Fonicettis tonight. I accepted on our behalf.'

'You did?' Bernie wondered how they had become a pair again. Two nights of torrid love-making and was the divorce supposed to be a past memory?

'He's invited Nico Constantine too, will you tell him please – there's no answer from his suite.'

Bernie nearly choked on his danish. 'Why Nico?'

'Why not? Daddy likes Nico.'

Yes, and hates me, Bernie thought. The last time they had met had been just before the divorce. Carlos Brent had confronted him at the Beverly Hills Hotel in the Polo lounge.

'You kike bastard – all I need is the word from Susanna, and my boys' club will be playing catch with your balls. You're lucky she's not vindictive.'

Charming! They had not spoken nor met since.

'I don't know if Nico will want to make it,' Bernie hedged. 'He's gotten very involved with a girl here.'

'Who?' Susanna demanded.

'Some chick, I don't even know her name.'

'Well he can bring her, a date will be OK.'

'I'll try to reach him.'

Susanna yawned and giggled. 'Can you believe what's happened to us? Can you believe it, Bernie? My analyst will have a blue fit!'

To be truthful Bernie was finding it very hard to believe himself. One moment he and Susanna were the worst of enemies – the next – making love like randy soldiers on twenty-four-hour leave! He had to admit that for him she was the absolute greatest in bed, but a pain in the ass to live with. Carlos had spoiled the pants off her, that was why.

A chubby waitress came rushing over. 'Miss Brent,' she gushed. 'And what can I get for you today?'

Miss Brent. It had always been Miss Brent, never ever Mrs Darrell. And on a couple of memorable occasions – memorable because of the blazing fight that followed – he had even been addressed as Mr Brent.

'I dunno, Maggi,' she knew all of the elderly waitresses by name – she had been coming to the hotel her entire life. 'I think maybe a cheese danish, and a black coffee.'

Maggi beamed. 'Certainly, dear.'

'I was thinking,' Susanna said, turning to Bernie. 'Why don't you and Nico fly back to LA with me? I can use daddy's plane whenever I want. I thought maybe tomorrow . . . You could stay at the house, Starr would like that.'

Starr was their very beautiful four-year-old daughter. She was also Carlos Brent's only grandchild, and as such she was spoiled rotten, just like her mother.

'I don't know,' Bernie answered, his mind racing. 'I promised Nico I'd stay with him . . .'

Susanna shot him a dirty look. 'Whose hand would you sooner hold? Mine or Nico's?'

'Yours, of course.'

'Anyway, his new girlfriend seems to be doing a pretty good job of holding his. I haven't even seen him yet.'

'You know how it is.'

'I certainly do.' She pushed her tinted shades up into her hair and sighed, 'We must have been mad to have gotten divorced. Why did we do it?'

Did she really expect an answer?

Because you nagged the shit out of me, Susanna.

Because you required my balls to be your balls.

Because daddy daddy daddy is enough to drive anyone to divorce.

Bernie shrugged, 'I don't know.'

Susanna giggled, that 'I wanna get laid' look came into her eyes. 'Why don't we forget about lunch?' she suggested. 'Why don't we just toddle on upstairs and smoke a little tiny bit of grass.'

'Yeah, why not.'

He certainly had nothing else to do with his time while he waited for Nico to surface.

13

'Who *was* he?' asked Vanessa.

'Some boring little con artist,' snapped Fontaine.

'He didn't look little to me, rather Omar Sharif actually.'

'A poor imitation.'

'You certainly left in a hurry, Paulo was furious.'

'Look, darling, I have to go, got a million things to do. I'll call you later.'

'Don't forget the fashion lunch tomorrow.'

'I've written it in my book.' Fontaine put the phone down, and checked out her appearance in the mirror. Chic, but understated. Silk shirt, pleated skirt, checked blazer. Just the outfit to interview aspiring managers for 'Hobo'. She had phoned Polly first thing and given her a blast. 'Get me some young, attractive, would-be front men. Franco's the reason "Hobo" is down the drain. Find me another Tony. I'll be over to see what you have at four o'clock.'

☆

Polly hung up the phone and snuggled up to Ricky. 'You'd better move it,' she said. 'Mrs K. is up early and raring to go.'

'She told me ten o'clock,' Ricky replied.

'In that case . . . we might just have time . . . Oh shit! I forgot. I'm the one with the early appointment.' She bounced out of bed. 'Any ideas on how I go about finding a tall sexy man with a big dick?'

Ricky laughed crudely. 'Don't I fit that bill?'

'Yes, you do. But you got the chauffeur's job, and Mrs K. would never understand a change of image midstream.'

'Why not? She seems like a pretty smart lady to me.'

'Oh, really?' Polly winked. 'Fancy her already, do you?'

He laughed. 'I wouldn't mind dipping my toe in.'

'She'd want more than your toe, sonny. Much more . . .'

'Why don't you come here and shut up.' Every time he thought about his employer he got quite randy.

☆

With the ring back in his possession Nico felt more secure. The delay had not been planned, and he imagined that Bernie must be worried by his silence. They had arranged that they would not make contact until he had actually fenced the ring and was on his way back.

But still, maybe he should call. Put Bernie's mind at rest. And then again, maybe not. Didn't want to alarm him unnecessarily. If all went well, and Hal came across, he could be on a plane within hours.

He delivered the ring personally to Hal the morning after his scene with Fontaine.

Hal wasn't pleased as he groped his way to the front door of his Park Lane service flat clad in a pair of black silk pyjamas. 'Jesus Christ!' he exclaimed, 'what the frig's the time?'

Nico glanced at his watch. 'Nine forty-five. Too early for you?'

'Too right it is. I never get up before two or three.'

'This is an emergency.'

'Yeah. I understand.' He led the way into an unused kitchen, and set about making some coffee. 'What happened? Fontaine throw you out early? Or didn't you get to stay?'

'I didn't stay.'

'Very wise. She's a balls-breaker.'

'Do you know her well?'

'Well enough.'

'Did you ever . . .'

'Me? Are you kidding?' Hal began to laugh. 'Fontaine wouldn't glance in my direction – not that I would ever want her to. She likes 'em young. When she was married to the Arab, she used his money to set them up in business.'

Nico produced the ring from his pocket and showed it to Hal.

Hal let out a long whistle. 'That's really something, absolutely bee-u-tiful.'

'When can I hear from you?' Nico asked. 'I have to be on my way as soon as possible.'

Hal poured water over instant coffee, already thinking of how he would spend his commission. 'A cash transaction like this . . . I should think some time tomorrow.'

'Christ!' Nico exclaimed, 'It has to be sooner than that.'

'I'll do my best, but there's a lot of money involved here. Just be patient and relax. Why don't you do some gambling? The London clubs are the best.'

Nico gave a hollow laugh. 'Why do you think I'm in trouble today?'

☆

'Hmmm . . . Not bad,' Fontaine yawned. 'What did you think, Polly?'

'I think that the cockney accent was just a little passé.'

Fontaine picked a nut from the glass dish on the table and tossed it into her mouth. 'Yes. I suppose you're right. Cockney was in last year – now it seems to be chinless or gay, but I *still* say what we need is a macho front man.'

'I know, I know, just like the fabulous Tony.'

Fontaine smiled dreamily. 'You never met him, did you?'

'I wish I had. But I was in America the year of "Hobo's" ascent.'

'Tony – at the beginning – was the best. In every way I might add.'

'So why did you get rid of him?'

'His ambitions screwed up his head.'

Polly and Fontaine sat together in the empty discothèque at 'Hobo' interviewing would-be managers. So far they had seen six, none of them suitable.

Fontaine was irritated, and getting more so by the minute. Why was it so goddamn difficult to find an attractive, ambitious, sexy, ballsy, young man?

She thought briefly of Jump Jennings. Thought even more briefly of importing him. Changed her mind, and peered at the next young man in line for the job.

He was better than the others. Curly black hair, tight faded jeans, a certain confidence.

Polly consulted a businesslike clipboard. 'And you are . . . ?'

'Steve Valentine.'

Fontaine and Polly exchanged quick amused looks.

'You're running a disco in Ealing?' Polly asked. 'Is that right?'

'I've been the manager there for eighteen months.'

'Do you enjoy it?' Fontaine husked, her kaleidoscope eyes inspecting every inch of him.

Steve stared at her. 'Yeah, well it's all right. But I want to get into the West End.'

'I'm sure you do.' Fontaine picked up a cigarette, and waited for him to light it.

He fumbled for a cheap lighter and did the honours.

'Hmmm . . .' said Fontaine, still inspecting him. 'Do you have a girlfriend?'

Steve's stare became bold. 'One wouldn't be enough for me, Mrs Khaled.'

'I bet it wouldn't.' She turned to Polly, 'I think we should give Mr Valentine a try, don't you, Polly?'

☆

When Nico left Hal's apartment he decided to make the most of his last day in London. He had in his possession the six thousand dollars that Bernie had withdrawn from his office safe – and apart from his hotel bill he would have no other expenses in London. By the time Hal disposed of the ring he would have more than enough cash to pay his debts in Vegas, repay Bernie, and still have a few thousand dollars over.

Of course, then he would have to start thinking of his

future. But he would worry about that when the time came. Also Mrs Dean Costello must be compensated, and that would be his responsibility if her insurance company had not already taken care of it. He had every intention of repaying her if she was not insured. How, he didn't quite know. But Nico had the quality of supreme confidence in his ability to deal with any situation. Plus the fact that no way would a ring like that be uninsured.

He thought about Fontaine Khaled. Flowers of course. Red roses naturally. Six dozen with a discreet note of apology. And a gift. Not the usual token trinket. But something nice and substantial. Something beautiful that she would love.

Even though he would be leaving London he had every intention of seeing her again. It was not inconceivable that he might return as soon as everything was settled.

Fontaine interested him like no other woman had since Lise Maria. He knew her, and yet he also knew that he had barely scratched the surface. She was a woman – arrogant, assured, tough. And underneath the veneer was the woman he really wanted to know. Vulnerable, soft, lovable. Searching for the right man – just as he – unknowingly – had been searching for the right woman.

He hailed a taxi and directed the driver to Boucheron, the Bond Street jewellery shop.

☆

Ricky watched Fontaine in the rear-view mirror as the Rolls glided through heavy traffic. Her eyes were closed, legs crossed, skirt riding up to reveal stocking tops. She wore suspenders! Christmas! Bloody suspenders! The only place he had ever seen those were in girly magazines!

He immediately felt randy – in spite of fifteen hot sticky minutes with Polly in the morning.

'Ricky.'

He shifted his eyes quickly to her face. She had woken up.

'Yes, Mrs Khaled.'

'Did you collect my things from the cleaners?'

'Yes, Mrs Khaled?'

'And pick up my prescription?'

'Yes, Mrs Khaled.'

'Good. When we get home you can take some time off. I won't be needing you until ten o'clock tonight.'

'Thank you, Mrs Khaled.' He glanced at the clock on the dashboard. It was nearly five. He was rather bushed himself. He sneaked another look in the mirror. She had pulled her skirt down. Spoilsport.

'Oh, and Ricky.'

'Yes, Mrs Khaled?'

'Be a good boy and keep your eyes on the road.'

'Yes, Mrs Khaled.'

Bitch!

☆

Nico enjoyed himself. He had always had a knack for spending money. Three thousand dollars went on a diamond-studded heart for Fontaine. Another thousand on a Carrier watch for Bernie. And twelve hundred on clothes for himself – cashmere sweaters and silk shirts from Turnbull & Asser.

Well pleased, he returned to his hotel.

Hal waited in the lobby. Things were progressing even faster than Nico had hoped.

'Good news?' he questioned.

'Let's go upstairs,' Hal replied.

They travelled up to Nico's suite in silence.

Once inside Hal produced the diamond ring and flung it down on the bed. 'Glass – fuckin' glass!' He spat in disgust. 'What the hell kind of game are you playin', Nico?'

14

Bernie was stoned. Nicely so. Just enough to be able to face Carlos Brent and the Fonicettis with a smile.

He prepared to leave Susanna at six o'clock with the promise to collect her at seven.

She lay in bed, also stoned, and suggested for the sixth time that they should get married again.

'Why?' Bernie asked. 'We're having such a good time together *not* being married.'

'I know,' agreed Susanna. 'But for Starr's sake it would be nice.'

Not to mention Carlos, Bernie thought. Big daddy would be furious if he knew what was going on.

'Don't forget to invite Nico,' Susanna called out after him.

'If he's around,' Bernie replied.

'He must be back by now. Who is the new girlfriend anyway?'

'I told you, I don't know. See you later.'

Bernie made his escape and returned to the suite.

Wouldn't it be nice if Nico was waiting to greet him.

He wasn't.

Bernie wondered if a phone call was in order. He certainly wanted to know what was happening. How much longer could he keep up the pretence that Nico was around? Of course he couldn't risk phoning from the Forum. He would have to stroll over to Caesars or Circus Circus and use an anonymous phone booth. He hoped to Christ that Nico had checked into the Lamont in London as he had told him to.

He took a shower and changed his clothes. Then he sprayed his mouth with a fresh breath spray, and set off to make the phone call.

☆

Cherry twirled in front of the full-length mirror. 'Do you like it?' she asked Dino breathily.

'Pretty,' he replied, more concerned with how the evening would go, than Cherry's new dress.

'You don't like it,' she pouted.

'Honey, I do,' he caught her up in his arms and hugged her reassuringly. 'You look like a great big beautiful doll.'

'I'm your wife,' she said proudly. 'Mrs Dino Foncetti!'

His stomach turned over with fear. In the entire thirty-one years he had been alive he had never made one important decision without consulting his father. Now he had really done it. He had sneaked off that very afternoon and married Cherry before Joseph thought of some smart way of getting rid of her.

'Your father's going to like me,' Cherry said, as if reading his mind. 'You'll see, he really will. I can promise you that.'

'I know, I know. Just keep your pretty mouth closed about us being married. I'll tell him in my own way.'

'Tonight?'

'Yeah, sure, tonight.'

She smiled. 'What a surprise it'll be! Me and your father meeting for the first time to talk about you and me getting married – and then boom – you'll tell him!'

'Yeah – boom.' Dino tried to smile. It was a struggle.

☆

Joseph Fonicetti arrived in the Magna Carter restaurant precisely at six forty-five. He inspected the dinner table, pronounced it suitable, and the head waiter sighed with relief.

Working for Joseph Fonicetti you learned to be meticulous.

'Bring me some Perrier water,' Joseph requested. 'And some of those little white cards.'

The waiter responded immediately, then stood at a respectful distance while Joseph scrawled in his atrocious handwriting on the placement cards.

At exactly two minutes to seven, David, the eldest son, arrived with his wife, Mia. They both embraced Joseph, and took their places at the table. They both ordered Perrier water to drink.

At exactly two minutes past seven Dino arrived with Cherry. He was holding her hand, but his palm was sweating so badly that her hand threatened to slip away.

'Cherry, I want you to meet my father, Joseph Fonicetti,' he said nervously.

Cherry stepped forward, wide-eyed. 'Mr Fonicetti, I have been *so* looking forward to this moment.'

Joseph beamed, 'So have I, my dear, so have I.' The girl was prettier than he had expected. Dino had always gone for the sour-faced big-boobed kind before. 'Sit right here, next to me. What'll you have to drink?'

Cherry's eyes didn't waver, but she had already noticed the Perrier bottles. 'Oh, Perrier water if I may – you don't mind, do you?'

'Mind? Of course not.' Smarter than he had expected.

Dino went to sit beside her.

Joseph waved him away. 'Down there, next to your sister-in-law.'

Dino moved obediently to the other end of the table and ordered a double scotch.

Susanna and Bernie arrived next, He did a double take when he saw Cherry. A part of the family? So soon?

Susanna rushed to kiss Joseph. 'Uncle Joe, you look younger every time I see you.' She blew kisses at David and Dino. They had been friends since childhood.

Then Carlos Brent made his entrance. A typical Carlos Brent entrance with noise and excitement and an entourage of six.

The dinner party was almost complete.

'Where's Nico Constantine?' asked Joseph. 'It's nearly a quarter after seven.'

Anyone who knew Joseph at all knew he was a stickler for punctuality.

Susanna looked at Bernie. 'Where *is* Nico?'

Bernie shrugged and tried to look suitably casual. 'He sent his apologies, hopes to make it later for coffee.'

'He's got a new girlfriend,' Susanna announced, 'I don't think she ever lets him out of bed!'

Joseph turned to Cherry. 'You're a friend of Nico's, aren't you?'

She smoothed down the front of her new pink dress. 'Nico's been like a father to me,' she said demurely.

I bet, thought Joseph. He was on to Cherry. Miss sweetness and light. She had dazzled Dino with the first clean pussy he had seen in years.

He wondered what it would take to get rid if her. Maybe Nico would know – after all he had brought her into Dino's life, and he could take her right on out again.

She was amazingly pretty. Bad wife material. She'd be screwing around before the ink was dry on the marriage licence.

Joseph glanced down the table at Mia. Now *that* was wife material.

'Mr Fonicetti,' Cherry gushed, 'You don't know how exciting this all is for me . . . Meeting Dino . . . you . . .'

'Where are you from, dear?' Joseph asked. May as well find out her version of her background before he put a private detective on to her.

☆

As far as Bernie was concerned the dinner dragged on for ever.

He needed it like he needed piles.

Susanna playing girl wife again. Carlos throwing him fishy dago false smiles. Mia and David both as dull as each other. Dino a nervous wreck. And Cherry – little Miss Blue Eyes – all innocence and golden curls and not fooling crafty old Joseph Fonicetti one bit.

Bernie had been unable to contact Nico in London. No answer in his hotel room. So he had left a message relaying the fact that everything was fine – so far. But how long before it was noticed that Nico's handsome face was no longer in evidence? And how long could Bernie fool them with a mystery girlfriend who didn't even exist?

As if on cue, Joseph said, 'Hey, Bernie, where's Nico? I thought you said he'd be here for coffee.'

'I guess he got hung up . . .'

'I invite people for dinner, they usually come. I want to talk to Nico . . . Business . . . Have him come up to my suite later.'

Oh, sure. Just like that. Bernie was beginning to seriously consider the possibility of jetting back to LA the next day with Susanna. Get out while he was clean.

'If I see him,' he said lamely. 'Like he's taken off with this girl . . .'

'Taken off?' Joseph snapped. 'Dino, did you hear that?'

'What?' Dino jumped. His mind had been exploring the possibility of a honeymoon in Europe, far far away from his father.

'Nico Constantine has taken off,' Joseph said grimly.

'Not taken off,' Bernie attempted a weak laugh. 'I mean he's around, but this girl . . . Well, you know how it can be . . .'

'What girl?' Joseph inquired, his eyes suddenly steely.

'I don't know her name . . .'

'Does she work here?'

'No, I don't think so.'

'So who is she? What does she do?'

Susanna joined in, 'Yes, who is this woman of mystery?'

Bernie could have belted her. He didn't like the look in Joseph's eyes. He was one smart old man.

'I told you, I don't know. Some broad who's dragged him away from the tables all the way into her bed.'

'Everyone!' Cherry clapped her hands excitedly, 'I can't keep it to myself any longer! Today, this very afternoon! Dino and I got married!'

Bernie could have kissed her. It was one heck of a good way to take everyone's mind off of Nico.

15

'What?' Nico could not believe what Hal was telling him.

'Glass,' Hal stated flatly, 'one helluva chunk of beautifully cut glass – set in real platinum of course. A copy – a beaut – but the real thing it ain't.'

'I don't believe it!' Nico felt an insane desire to laugh. 'I just don't believe it!'

'Start believing, kid. It's not worth more than a few hundred.'

Nico shook his head in amazement. So – Mrs Dean Costello had fooled him. Or had she? The old dear had never claimed that her ring was real. She had never handed him papers to prove its authenticity. She probably had the real thing locked up in a bank vault. Of course. It was obvious. A diamond that size – all the rich women had copies made of their gems. And excellent copies too. Good enough to fool everyone except the experts.

Nico was embarrassed. 'Hal, what can I say? I had no idea . . .'

Hal was friendly. 'Of course you didn't. Even I thought it was the real thing, and I have an eye – I can spot the real stuff a mile off. Listen, it was nice nearly doing business with you.' He prepared to leave. 'Give my best to Bernie. Will you be leaving today?'

Nico shrugged, 'I don't know what I'm going to do.'

'You know what you really need? A rich, old broad.' Hal laughed, 'Rich, old, and grateful.' He warmed to his subject. 'Now I have a couple of hot ones flying in from Texas tomorrow. You want a million dollars – no problem. But you'll have to work for it . . .'

'How old?'

'Not spring chickens . . .'

'How old?'

'In their sixties, maybe creeping up to seventy . . . But you'd never know, what with silicone tits and face jobs and . . .'

'Forget it.'

'Suit yourself, but it's a winning game.'

Yeah. A winning game. That's what he really needed.

Hal left, and Nico paced his hotel room wondering what his next move should be. Alert Bernie. That had to be first. Tell him to get out of Vegas and stop covering up for him.

Then what? How was he ever going to get half a million dollars?

How had he ever lost half a million dollars?

Gambling.

His bankroll was almost non-existent, but that didn't phase him. He picked up the phone and requested the Manager.

Full Nico charm. 'Mr Graheme, I have a slight problem, my bank in Switzerland is transferring funds – by tomorrow no problem. In the meantime if you could let me have – say – five hundred pounds cash – and charge it to my bill I would be most grateful . . .'

☆

The six dozen red roses arrived late afternoon. They were waiting for Fontaine when she returned to her house after the auditions. Mrs Walters had set them out in matching cut glass vases.

'Christ!' Fontaine exclaimed irritably. 'The place is beginning to look like a funeral parlour! I know I asked for fresh flowers Mrs Walters, but this is ridiculous.'

Mrs Walters clucked her agreement, and handed her employer the card which had accompanied the roses.

Fontaine read it. The message was brief – just – 'Thank you. Nico.'

Thank you for what? For a great screw? For throwing him out? For what?

Fontaine tore the card into tiny pieces and let it flutter over the carpet.

Mrs Walters pursed her lips. Who would have to clear *that* up later.

'I don't want to be disturbed,' Fontaine sighed. 'I simply have to rest.'

'Your lawyer has telephoned three times, Mrs Khaled, he says it's urgent that he arrange an appointment with you immediately.'

'How boring.'

'And Count Rispollo telephoned.'

'Even more boring.'

'What shall I say if they phone again, Mrs Khaled?'

'Tell them I am resting, and to telephone tomorrow.'

'Oh, and this arrived.' Mrs Walters produced a small package.

Fontaine took it from her and balanced it in her hand. Boucheron. Was it a token of Count Paulo's esteem?

'Wake me at eight o'clock.' She walked upstairs.

The thought occurred that maybe she should have brought Steve Valentine home with her. Personally seen to it that he had what it takes in all the right places.

Once that would have been exciting. But somehow the thrill of just another horny body was beginning to pall.

Now Nico . . .

Screw Nico . . . She didn't even want to think about him. Lousy hustler. Using her to smuggle his stuff through customs. Sharing her bed only to recover his ring.

She ripped open the packet from Boucheron, and read the card that fell out.

Same card. Same message. 'Thank you. Nico.'

Thoughtfully she stared at the diamond-encrusted heart. It was very lovely. She took it out of the box and held it in her hand.

Nico . . . He *had* been a very special lover . . .

☆

So far so good. Nico was winning. Nothing sensational – but a beginning.

He had started the evening with a stake of a thousand pounds – this he had managed to work up to twenty-five thousand pounds. A nice beginning.

For a change everything seemed to be going his way. And if his luck kept right on . . . Who knew what could happen?

He was enjoying the ambience of a British gaming club. So different from the brashness of Vegas.

Delightful female croupiers in low-cut dresses. Discreet pit bosses. Respectful girls serving unobtrusive drinks.

The atmosphere was that of a rather elegant club.

Nico lit up a long thin cigar, and moved from a blackjack table to roulette. The limit was not as high as he would have wished, and he was unable to bet more than five hundred on black. It came up. Good. But certainly not good enough. He needed to get into a high stake poker game, and he looked around for someone who might be able to arrange it.

The manager seemed a likely prospect, and sure enough he was. He recommended another club which would be happy to accommodate Nico as far as poker, backgammon, whatever he wished.

Nico took a taxi there.

He had tried to telephone Bernie earlier, but had been unable to reach him. Now he just wanted to concentrate on making some sort of big score.

☆

'Hmmm . . .' Fontaine stood in the doorway and surveyed the disco at 'Hobo'. 'Well I suppose I mustn't expect miracles. It *is* his first night.'

Polly nodded. 'He looks good though, don't you think?'

Fontaine watched Steve through narrowed kaleidoscope eyes. 'He doesn't have the walk.'

'What walk?'

'The John Travolta cock thrust. You know what I mean, Polly.'

Polly couldn't help giggling. Cock thrust. It sounded like something you did in an aeroplane!

Steve came towards them. He was clad in a rather cheap black pinstripe suit, shirt, and tie.

'Mrs Khaled. A table for how many?'

'The look is wrong, Steve,' she snapped. 'You're running a disco – not your uncle's wedding!'

'Sorry.'

'Don't worry, I should have told you. Obviously they're a touch more formal in Ealing. Now, let me see . . .'

She reached for his tie, undid and removed it. Then she unbuttoned his shirt three buttons. 'That's better. Tomorrow I'll take you out shopping.'

Oh God! Shades of Tony! How well she remembered their first meeting. A disaster. He had possessed an animal charm, a sexy walk, but that was about all. And in bed – nothing but raw ability.

She had seen his potential, and trained him to make full use of it in every way.

He had learned quickly. And then he had got far too big for his newly acquired Gucci loafers.

Now Steve stood before her. Raw material. Was it worth building him into a monster too?

Count Paulo, who was lucky enough to be escorting Polly and Fontaine, gave Steve a dirty look. 'Mrs Khaled's table?'

'Of course,' Steve jumped to attention.

Count Paulo ordered the obligatory champagne, and asked Fontaine to dance.

'You dance with him Polly,' Fontaine commanded. 'At least try and make the place look busy.'

☆

Nico's run of luck continued to the tune of fifty thousand pounds. He was smart enough to quit as soon as the cards began to turn.

He felt elated . . . so elated that he risked a phone call to Fontaine.

A disgruntled housekeeper – obviously woken from a deep sleep – informed him that madam was out.

Then he spotted the girl again. A very tall blonde in a very stark dress. He had noticed her earlier in the evening at the other gaming club. She was certainly striking. Not a fresh-faced beauty nor a sophisticated Fontaine. But very very striking . . .

She smiled at him across the room, and he smiled back.

He thought no more about her.

He collected his coat from reception, tipped the man at the desk handsomely, and signalled the doorman for a cab.

She appeared just as he was climbing in. 'Can you give me a lift?' Her voice was soothingly husky. 'I am escaping from an over-amorous Arab, and if I don't vanish immediately I'm in trouble.'

Nico raised a quizzical eyebrow. 'You are?'

'Please?'

'Hop in. I always help beautiful women in trouble.'

She smiled. 'I knew you'd say that.'

'You did?'

'You look like Omar Sharif – so why shouldn't you sound like him.'

'I'm not an Arab, I'm Greek.'

'I know that. There's no way I would've shared a taxi with an Arab, thank you.'

'How did you know I was Greek?'

She opened her purse, took out a compact, and inspected her face. 'I didn't know *what* you were . . . I just knew you weren't an Arab.' She clicked the compact shut. 'Hi – I'm Lynn.' Formally she extended her hand. 'And you?'

'Nico Constantine.'

'Greek name, but you sound American.'

'Yes, I've lived in LA for the last ten years. Now – where can I drop you?'

Lynn mock pouted, 'Trying to get rid of me so soon . . .'

Nico laughed, 'Not at all.'

'Did I hear you tell the cab driver the Lamont?'

'That's where I'm staying.'

'They only do the best scrambled eggs in town, don't they.'

'They do?'

'If you don't know you must try.'

The restaurant will be closed . . .'

'And room service will be open . . .'

☆

Vanessa, Leonard, and a whole group of people arrived at 'Hobo' as Fontaine's guests.

She watched the women's reactions to Steve. Nothing special.

'Do you fancy him?' she whispered to Vanessa.

'He's not Tony.'

'*Fuck* Tony. I'm sick to death of hearing about Tony. He's not the only stud in the world you know.' Fontaine drained her champagne glass, and gestured for more.

'He *is* quite cute . . .' Vanessa ventured.

'Cute! Christ! That's hardly what I'm looking for.'

The evening sped by in a haze of champagne. Fontaine allowed herself to get delightfully, pleasantly bombed.

Count Paulo clutched her in his arms on the dance floor and declared undying love and lust. 'We must be in bed together soon,' he panted, 'my whole body screams for you.'

He rubbed embarrassingly against her, and she wished he'd take his juvenile Italian horniness back to Italy with him.

She danced with Leonard.

'How about a cosy lunch one day, just the two of us?' he suggested.

God save her from the middle-aged husbands who considered her fair game.

Goodbyes were said in the early hours of the morning on the pavement outside 'Hobo'.

Ricky stood obediently holding the door of the Rolls open while Fontaine, Polly, and Count Paulo piled in.

'Drop Miss Brand first,' Fontaine ordered. 'Then Count Rispollo.'

'Yes, Mrs Khaled.'

Polly managed a surreptitious wink as she was dropped off. 'Later?' she whispered.

'You bet,' Ricky replied, *sotto voce*.

Count Paulo was complaining loudly about being

driven to his hotel. 'Tonight I thought we would be together,' he said bitterly. 'I come all the way to see you – and you treat me like . . . like dirt.'

'I'm tired,' Fontaine replied coolly. 'Maybe tomorrow. Call me.'

A disappointed Count Paulo was deposited outside his hotel.

'Home, Ricky,' instructed Fontaine.

He glanced at the clock. Four o'clock in the bleedin' morning. He hoped she wasn't expecting him bright and early at ten a.m. By the time he made it back to Polly's and gave her a good seeing to . . . Well, he'd need some sleep, wouldn't he?

They arrived at Fontaine's Pelham Crescent house. Ricky jumped out of the Rolls and held the door open for her.

She yawned openly and sighed. Dawn was beginning to break. Her kaleidoscope eyes swept over him. 'Coming in for an early morning cup of tea, Ricky?'

☆

Nico and Lynn made love in his hotel suite. A room service trolley bearing two plates of congealed scrambled eggs stood forlornly in the centre of the living room.

Lynn was accomplished, striking, pleasant.

The sex was enjoyable.

Nico wished he hadn't.

She was just another female. A beautiful body – yes. But a stranger. And somehow sex with strangers was not the way he wanted to lead his life anymore. He was too old for one-night stands. And too smart. And he wished he was with Fontaine beneath her black silk sheets exchanging lives.

'That was good,' Lynn said, getting up from the bed.

'Very good,' Nico agreed, hoping she would dress and go.

She stretched, naked and cat-like. 'Are you into bondage?'

'What?'

'Bondage. You know, being tied up and beaten. The Arabs love it.'

'I told you, I'm not an Arab.'

'I know.' She arched her back, then touched her toes. Her body was somewhat sinewy. 'You're a Greek who talks American.' She picked up her dress from the floor and started to pull it on. 'And you're also a dumb son-of-a-bitch who had better pay back the money you owe the Fonicettis or you're going to find yourself an unrecognizable son-of-a-bitch. Am I making myself clear?'

'What did you say?' Nico sat up in bed, shocked.

Lynn fiddled with the zipper on her dress. Her smoky voice was very sensuous. 'You heard me. I'm a messenger, so you had better listen very very carefully.' She searched for her spike-heeled shoes and put them on. 'You have a week, seven days, no credit. Understand?' She picked up her purse and moved towards the door. She paused and smiled. 'Every cent, Nico, or . . . well . . . they're going to cut your balls off, and wouldn't that be a shame?'

She exited, closing the door quietly behind her.

☆

'Isn't this fun?' Fontaine watched Ricky through slitted eyes as he poured the tea.

He wasn't sure whether to answer or not. In fact he didn't know how to act at all.

'You know,' Fontaine murmured thoughtfully, 'you're really rather sexy. Why didn't I think of using *you* for the club?'

'Sugar, Mrs Khaled?'

'No, thank you,' she turned her back on him. 'Bring the tea up to the bedroom, Ricky, yours as well.'

He stood in the kitchen and watched her go. Then quick as a flash he whipped out a tray and put the two cups of tea on it. 'Ricky m'boy,' he muttered to himself, 'I think you just got lucky.'

'Ricky,' her slightly drunken voice called from the top of the stairs, 'are you coming?'

Of course he was. Polly would just have to wait.

16

Bernie, Susanna, and Cherry sat in silence aboard Carlos Brent's private plane. Each one of them in deep thought.

Susanna smiled slightly. The shit had hit – Bernie's charming expression – but it hadn't flown in her direction.

Cherry sobbed quietly, occasionally dabbing at her baby-blue eyes with a silk monogrammed handkerchief taken from one of Dino's drawers.

Bernie sat stoically. Mr Fall Guy. Mr Schmuck. It was just good luck he was connected to Carlos Brent, even if it was only a fragile connection. If he hadn't been . . .

If Susanna had not intervened on his behalf . . .

Well, he didn't like to think what would have happened.

Bernie reflected on the previous evening's happenings. It all seemed like a bad fucking dream.

First it was pure shit-luck that Joseph Fonicetti had decided to throw a dinner party. Second, the fact that Nico was an invited guest. And third, that Cherry and Dino had sneaked off and gotten married.

What a joke *that* was.

The whole mix was disaster time.

Joseph Fonicetti was far too canny an old animal to let anything slide past him. And the fact that Nico owed –

and owed big – was reason enough for him to be suspicious when Nico failed to show.

Of course, when Cherry announced the fact that she and Dino were married the party really took off.

Joseph Fonicetti did not like surprises – especially of that kind. And he had risen from the table, small mean eyes burning in his nut brown face. 'Is this fuckin' true?' he had screamed at Dino, down the table. 'Are you gonna tell me you've *married* the dumb cunt?'

Cherry had joined in then, blue eyes tearful but determined. 'How dare you call me that – *how dare you*!' Appealingly she had looked to Dino for support.

Dino had slunk down in his chair. How could he argue with his father? The unfortunate truth was that she *was* a dumb cunt for opening up her mouth.

'Get me Nico Constantine, cut out the bullshit and find him,' Joseph demanded.

Bernie had visibly blanched. He did not know what to say.

Joseph sensed this immediately. 'He *is* still here, isn't he, Bernie?' The voice was menacing.

Susanna cut in quickly with – 'Of course he is, Uncle Joe.'

Joseph ignored her. 'Check it out, David. I want that son-of-a-bitch, Nico, and I want him now.' He indicated a by now sobbing Cherry. 'She's his – this . . . this Barbie doll! He can take her right on out of our lives.'

'Mr Fonicetti!' Cherry had gulped. 'Dino and I are *married*.'

'Find out where the stupid fuck did it, and take care of that too, David,' Joseph snapped. 'And get me Nico –

pronto. There's also the matter of the money he owes us. Dino was supposed to take care of that – but he's been too busy taking care of his cock.' At this point Joseph had burst into a stream of angry Italian – a language that had stayed with him since childhood.

Carlos Brent had risen from the table, gone to Joseph, and put his arm around him.

The dinner party was over.

So was Cherry and Dino's marriage.

So was Nico when they found out he had split.

And so was Bernie when they found out he had aided and abetted.

Quickly he had put his arm around Susanna, 'Let's get married again,' he suggested. 'We've had such a great time this last couple of days.'

'Anything to save your ass, huh Bernie?' But she grinned when she said it.

Naturally it did not take them long to find out that Nico was gone.

Bernie had been hauled up to the Fonicetti penthouse for questioning. Susanna had insisted on accompanying him.

To save his own ass he was forced to tell them where Nico was.

'We'll take care of it,' Joseph had muttered ominously.

'He only went so he could raise the money to pay you,' Bernie insisted. 'He's probably on his way back now.'

'Sure, sure.' Joseph stared him down with his mean little eyes. 'Remember one thing in your life, Bernie. Loyalty. But don't fuck it up. Loyalty to the *right* people.

When you knew Nico couldn't pay you should have come to me immediately. No hesitation. You understand?'

Bernie nodded vigorously.

'But . . . you're young . . . you have a lot to learn. And I myself have loyalty to Carlos Brent. So you are lucky. You understand?'

'He understands, Uncle Joe,' Susanna kissed the old man on the cheek. 'It won't happen again. And thank you.'

So Bernie's balls were intact. Only thing was, they now belonged to Susanna again.

☆

Cherry shared an apartment in Hollywood with two other girls. They were both away. One on a fishing trip with a porno-movie star. The other on location in Oregon.

Cherry wandered around the empty apartment in a daze. It had all happened so quickly. One moment she was Mrs Dino Fonicetti. The next – just plain Cherry, unsuccessful actress.

It wasn't fair. What was wrong with her? What made her unsuitable material to be Dino's wife? Why did his father automatically hate her?

She stared at her exquisite reflection in the mirror. Blonde hair. Blue eyes. Perfect features. With Dino's dark good looks, what beautiful babies they would have made together.

Dino. His behaviour had not been very nice. Allowing his father to call her horrible names.

She gave a long drawn-out sigh, walked in the tiny bathroom, removed a line of drying underclothes from across the bath, selected her favourite bubbles, and started to run the water.

Then she stripped off her clothes and stepped into the bath.

☆

'Operator, try that number again please.' Bernie bounced his daughter Starr on his knee, and tried to locate Nico for the fifth time.

Susanna was busy unpacking his clothes. On the way from the airport she had insisted on picking up all his things, from Nico's rented house.

'We can do it tomorrow,' Bernie had complained.

'Now. I want to feel you're really back. Not just sharing my bed for a night.'

As she unpacked she complained, 'Look at these shirts! My God what kind of a laundry did you send these to!

'Bernie, these socks should have been thrown away, they're full of holes.

'Oh no! This is my favourite sweater and you've got a cigarette burn in it. How could you?'

Bernie tuned out, and concentrated on reaching Nico. The least he could do was warn him.

'I think we should have a small wedding, nothing flashy, something tasteful, with Starr as a bridesmaid. What do you think, Bernie?'

'Good idea.'

'Daddy suggested his house in Palm Springs. We could fly everyone up. That would be fun, wouldn't it?'

'Sure.' Goddamn daddy again.

'And I'll wear blue – and how about you in a blue suit

so that we match? And Starr in blue frills. Oh Bernie, it's all so exciting!'

There was nothing Susanna liked better than planning a party – or a wedding for that matter. Bernie remembered with a feeling of dread their famous Saturday night intimate dinner parties for fifty or sixty. Shit. This time he would have to put his foot down.

'We're ringing Mr Constantine's suite,' the hotel operator's voice said.

Three rings and Nico answered.

'I've been trying to reach you for days,' Bernie exclaimed. 'The shit has—

17

'Hit. I know.' Nico replied.

'How do you know? What's happened?' Bernie stuttered.

'They have given me a very generous seven days to come up with the money.'

'And the ring?'

'Glass, my friend.'

'What'll you do?'

'I'll think of something.'

'Listen, Nico. It wasn't my fault they found out. I tried. I kept it going for days. What happened is a long story.'

'Save it. I'll be back to hear it personally. In one piece, I hope.'

'I'm glad you can take it so calmly.'

'What other way is there?'

'If you need me I'm at Susanna's.'

'Reconciliation?'

'I'll explain.'

'Keep hold of your balls.'

'You too.'

Nico hung up the phone. He *was* calm. His energies could not be wasted on panicking. He had sat and thought from the moment of Lynn's departure.

There were two moves that he could make. One – take his fifty thousand pounds winnings and escape. South America, Athens . . . Change his name, start a new life. The snag was he had no particular desire to change his name and life.

Two – pay them the money he owed. If he could somehow raise it that was.

Two was the only answer of course. But how?

He fell asleep still trying to work it out.

☆

Fontaine awoke to the smell and a taste of a hangover, and a hammering on her locked bedroom door.

Oh God! She felt positively dreadful.

'Mrs Khaled,' the voice assaulted her, 'it's past twelve, I have your breakfast tray.'

'Leave it outside, Mrs Walters.'

Oh God! Her headache was lethal. She tried to remember fragments of the previous evening – and did.

Oh God! Ricky. He was still asleep in her bed. She sat up and surveyed the room. It looked like a party had taken place.

Oh God! It had. Just the two of them. Talk about shades of Lady Chatterley's lover!

She slid from the bed into a silk kimono, and thought about how to get rid of him.

Mrs Walters wouldn't be shocked that she had had a man spend the night, she was used to that. But the fact that it was her chauffeur! Oh God!

'Ricky,' she gave him a short sharp shove. 'Kindly get up and piss off.'

'What? What?' He opened his eyes. 'Where am I?' Then he remembered. 'Oh – yes, 'course. C'm here darlin', I'll give you a bit more of what you enjoyed last night.'

She withered him with a look. 'Forget about last night, Ricky. And I am not darling, I am Mrs Khaled, and don't you forget it. Now kindly dress and get the hell out of here.'

He sat up in bed. 'Are you giving me the old elbow?'

'If you mean am I firing you, the answer is no. But just remember, last night was a figment of your imagination.'

Bloody hell! Some figment. He had a very good recollection of Mrs Khaled sitting astride him in nothing but a mink coat and his chauffeur's cap yelling, 'First one to the gate is the winner!' Bloody hell!

Fontaine retired into the bathroom, and Ricky dressed quickly. He let himself out of the locked bedroom, nearly tripped over the breakfast tray, and sneaked downstairs.

Mrs Walters was busy dusting. She gave him a look of disdain and a disgusted sniff.

'Morning Mrs Walters.'

She turned her back on him.

☆

Backgammon had always been a game Nico excelled at. He presented himself at a London club and exercised his skills. London had no lack of backgammon hustlers, but Nico was more than a match for them.

He spent the afternoon at play, and emerged in the early evening a few thousand pounds richer.

Not bad, but not nearly enough to even begin to help.

He needed advice. He called Hal.

They met in 'Trader Vics' for a drink, Hal resplendent in a new white suit.

Nico fingered the lapel. 'Looks good.'

'Gotta be my best for the ladies. They're here. If I play it right I could well own half of Detroit by tomorrow morning! Sure you wouldn't like to join us for dinner?'

'If they have five hundred thousand dollars to hand my way . . .'

Hal laughed. 'Five years solid fucking could probably get you that.'

Nico grimaced. 'I need it a little sooner.' His black eyes fixed on to Hal, almost hypnotic in their intensity. 'I am deadly serious about needing the money, Hal. I blew out of Vegas owing. Thought the ring would cover it. Now' – he made a gesture of hopelessness – 'they've found me. They sent a woman messenger. I thought she was a beautiful girl looking to get laid. She got laid all right – and then she delivered the message. Seven days. They mean business – you know it and I know it. Do you have any suggestions?'

Hal summoned the pretty Chinese waitress and ordered another Navy Grog. He was sympathetic. But not *that* sympathetic. He liked Nico very much. But if trouble was coming he wanted to be long gone.

'Let me get some details here,' he said, stalling for time while he thought of a fast excuse to be on his way. 'Who do you owe? And how much?'

'I wasn't kidding you. I owe the Fonicettis five hundred and fifty grand.'

Hal let out a long low whistle, 'Jeez! I know old Joe

Fonicetti. Are you gonna tell me they let you run up markers for that much? It's impossible.'

'Not when you lose six hundred thou of your own money up front.'

Hal whistled again. 'You are in trouble, my friend. Big big trouble.'

The Chinese girl brought his drink, and smiled inscrutably at both of them.

'I've never fucked a Chinese,' Hal said absently as she walked away. 'Now tell me, Nico. Who was your lady messenger? Did they send somebody over?'

Nico shook his head. 'She was English. Said her name was Lynn.'

'Very tall? Good body?'

Nico nodded. 'You know her?'

'She used to be a dancer on TV. Never made it out of the back line until she met the man himself.'

'What man?'

'Feathers. Lynn's his right-hand woman. One tough lady – expert judo – the martial arts – you were lucky you only got fucked!'

'Thanks a lot.'

'I wish I could talk to Feathers,' Hal mused aloud. 'Maybe we could figure out something . . .'

'Why can't you?' Nico asked.

'We're not on the best of terms right now. A debt. It's dragged on.'

'How much?'

'Five thousand pounds. I keep him happy with a payment here a payment there. But he'd be a lot happier to see a lump sum.'

'Pay him the lump sum. I have it. Call it a fee for your help.'

'Hey, Nico. You don't have to do that.'

'I know I don't. But if you can work out some deal with Feathers – that *he* can work out with Fonicetti. Maybe an instalment plan like you had . . . What do you think?'

Hal nodded slowly. 'Whatever I can do, I'll do.'

Nico patted him on the shoulder. 'Thanks. I'll appreciate anything you can manage.'

☆

Wild-looking model girls in exotic underclothes undulated frantically down the catwalk.

Fontaine, at a ringside table, openly yawned.

'Aren't you enjoying it?' Vanessa asked anxiously. The fashion show was raising money for one of her charities and she desperately wanted it to be a success.

'I never did get turned on gaping at other women's bodies,' Fontaine replied, 'Aren't there any *male* models? You know – horny little nineteen-year-olds in nothing but their jockeys and a smile?'

'Oh Fontaine! Really! It's the clothes you're supposed to be looking at.'

'Hmmm . . .' Fontaine allowed her gaze to wander around the restaurant where the fashion show was taking place. Tables and tables of boring women, all dressed in the latest most expensive clothes. Just as she was.

God! Was this what her life was all about? Fashion and Getting Fucked. Both were beginning to pall.

'I have to leave soon,' she whispered to Vanessa. 'Got to meet with my lawyer. Boring old Arnold is threatening me with the workhouse if I don't come up with some money soon. That pittance Benjamin pays me hardly covers my weekly expenses. I simply *have* to get "Hobo" back in action.'

'You will,' Vanessa replied. 'When you put your mind to it nothing can stop you.'

'I know, I know. I always get what I want. But don't you see, Vanessa, that's just an impression I create.'

Vanessa looked at her friend disbelievingly. She envied Fontaine her life, and could never imagine her being dissatisfied. All the women envied Fontaine's lifestyle – even if they pretended not to. She had beauty, freedom, and certainly no visible lack of money.

Vanessa had a rich husband, four children, an overweight figure, and not a moment to call her own.

Fontaine had a seemingly never-ending supply of fanciable young men.

Vanessa had only managed two affairs in twelve long years of marriage.

'I'm so bored!' Fontaine stated. 'Shall I tell you a secret, Vanessa? Just between you and me. Don't you *dare* tell anyone.'

Vanessa nodded, her eyes shining. Tell me! Tell me!' she pleaded.

'Last night, I was so bored that I screwed my chauffeur.'

'You didn't?!'

'I certainly did. And let me tell you it was even more boring than being bored!'

'What?' Vanessa frowned. 'Wasn't he any good?'

'All the attributes, my darling. Big cock, firm balls, and lovely thighs. But BORING!'

Vanessa blinked. Fontaine was the most outrageous outspoken person she had ever met.

'The thing is,' Fontaine continued, 'when I was married to Benjamin, all these little adventures seemed so much more exciting. Now . . . well . . . It's all so bloody predictable.'

'I've met someone—' Vanessa began.

Fontaine ignored her, and continued speaking. 'Now that man on the plane – Nico. Not my usual scene at all, darling. But I must say, with him, it was just . . . different. He was so . . . I don't know – it seems a silly word for me to use, but he was so worldly, *and* amusing. Maybe I made a mistake throwing him out.'

'I never did get to meet him—' Vanessa started to say.

They were interrupted by the arrival of Sammy at their table.

'Mornin' gels! Havin' a wonderful time?'

He sat himself down.

'Do have a seat,' Fontaine murmured.

'Ah, her highness is in form today.' He poured himself some wine. 'Listen darlin's, want you to take a look at my new collection.' He indicated the models, now in sports clothes. 'Anything you want – it's yours.'

'You're very generous today,' Fontaine said. 'Why?'

''Cos you're gorgeous, darlin'. Bit long in the tooth for me . . . but . . .'

'Piss off, Sammy,' Fontaine said mildly.

'No offence, my darlin'. I like 'em twenty. Everyone to their own. Know what I mean?'

Fontaine couldn't help smiling. Sammy was a genuine character, and a likeable one.

'Your clothes aren't my usual style,' she said.

'So – wear 'em at the beach. Big deal. Pick out what you want – it'll be good for me if you have 'em.'

Fontaine ticked off a halter jump suit on her programme, and a white track suit. Actually his designs were quite fun.

'So – ready for me to take over "Hobo" yet?' Sammy asked.

'I'll tell you what, Sammy, I *am* giving it serious thought.'

He laughed, 'Really?'

'Why not? You *are* Mr Personality.'

'Oh, yeah?'

'I think you could be quite an attraction. Not in the same way as Tony of course.'

'Oh, of course.'

'But in your own way . . .'

'Hey – hang on. I was only joking you know. I've got a business to run.'

Fontaine fixed him with her kaleidoscope eyes. 'Sammy?' she said briskly. 'How does the idea of becoming a *partner* in "Hobo" appeal to you?'

18

Bernie settled back into married life like a mouse into a trap.

Susanna gaily made second wedding plans, nagged him continually about this and that, and phoned dear old Carlos for a loving conversation at least twice a day.

'Find out what they're doing about Nico,' Bernie instructed.

'How can I?' Susanna replied innocently.

'Don't give me that shit,' Bernie snapped. 'You know, and *I* know, and so does all of Hollywood, that Carlos Brent – superstar supreme – has connections that make Watergate look like a kiddies' tea party. He probably owns the fucking Forum hotel for all we know.'

'Don't be ridiculous. Daddy's so called "connections" are in your head.'

'Bullfuckingshit. I want you to find Nico. He's a good friend of mine, and I don't want anything to happen to him.'

Shrilly, Susanna sniped, 'He didn't seem to care so much about what happened to *you*, did he? Left you holding the can, and if you and I hadn't gotten back together . . . Well, you *know* how daddy felt about your treatment of me.'

'Yes, I know. He'd have been only too pleased to have me pushing up cacti in the fucking desert.'

Susanna made a face. 'You're such a smartass, you really are. What a stupid thing to say.'

Two hours later she casually relayed the information that Nico had been allowed a week to pay.

'You see, Uncle Joseph is a kind and generous man.'

'Uncle Joseph! Only *you* would call one of the biggest mobsters in Vegas, Uncle.'

Susanna pursed her lips. 'The trouble with you, Bernie, is that you think everyone even remotely associated with Las Vegas is a gangster. Uncle Joseph is a perfectly respectable *hotel* owner.'

'Yeah, and the Pope's Jewish!'

Bernie waited until Susanna and Starr went out to order their wedding outfits, then he went up to the bedroom, and checked in Susanna's clothes closet to see if her safe was still there.

It was. Concealed behind a shoe rack.

It occurred to him that she might have had the combination changed. But as he twiddled the knob he realized it was the same.

The door swung open, and facing him was her myriad collection of jewellery boxes, each one containing a diamond encrusted gift from her father.

Also there were the one hundred thousand dollars in cash that Carlos had handed them as a wedding present.

One hundred neat, crisp, thousand-dollar bills. Untouched. Intact. And half his – although Susanna had never allowed him near it.

What kind of a schmuck hung onto *cash* when the

money could have been sitting in a bank accumulating interest?

His ex-soon-to-be-present-wife – dear Susanna.

'We'll keep it as emergency money,' she had stated five years before. And that was the last he had seen of it.

Susanna didn't even realize that he knew the safe's combination, but he had watched her fetch a necklace from it one night, and the numerals had stuck.

Well . . . half was his. He was entitled.

He extracted fifty one-thousand-dollar bills, and replaced them with singles at the bottom of the stack.

If he could help Nico with the money – he would.

19

Sammy said yes. Just like that.

He surprised everyone, including himself. But what was money for if not to spend it? And he had always had a hankering to front a club. It was the extrovert in him.

'I'm not another Ian Thaine tryin' to creep into your bed,' he warned Fontaine.

'God forbid!'

So they set a deal, shook hands, and then they were in business together.

For Fontaine it was a lifesaver. Her finances really were in a frightening state. She needed Hobo to be a success again.

Once involved, Sammy did not hang about. He hired incredible black sixteen-year-old twin disc jockeys – a girl and a boy. New waiters, all young, ambitious, and highly paid. He liked Steve Valentine, and decided to keep him on as a backup. He sent him to Leonard for a perm, and Bruno for an all-white wardrobe. The difference was startling.

'It's amazing, you've given him style,' Fontaine exclaimed.

''Course I have,' agreed Sammy. 'Now let's concentrate

on changing the menu, and getting a new light system going.'

Fontaine and Sammy were the odd couple. Working together until all hours. Planning, laughing, joking. To their mutual surprise they actually liked each other. Nothing sexual – purely platonic. Sammy was amazed at Fontaine's sense of humour. When she wasn't busy doing her bullshit sexy Mrs Khaled number, she was witty, down to earth, and a lot of fun to be with.

Fontaine found that she adored Sammy. He was warm and humorous and natural.

She was so busy that she even forgot about sex. At night she was happy to collapse into bed – alone – after a hard day at the club.

Sammy had decided they should close 'Hobo' down for a few days while they made their changes. Then reopen with a huge party. 'Expensive, but worth it my darlin',' he assured her.

She agreed. She didn't want to tell him that her lawyer was now suggesting she should sell her house and car to meet all the mounting debts. Her lawyer was an idiot. She would prove to him how wrong he was.

She forgot about her problems and launched into planning a really lavish party.

Champagne and caviar for two hundred of London's most fun people. What did a few more bills matter? In for a penny, in for the whole bloody lot.

☆

It took Hal almost a week to arrange a meeting between Nico and Feathers.

'He is not an easy man to get to see,' Hal explained. 'And a meet with one of his minions would do you no good at all. But don't worry, I've explained your situation, and he'll see you tonight.'

'Christ!' Nico exclaimed. 'Tomorrow my seven days are up. This is cutting it rather too fine for my nerves.'

'Feathers has connections in all the right places. I'm sure it'll be worked out. Don't forget, he's in direct contact with the Fonicettis – your debt is his concern now.'

Nico had spent an uneasy few days. His luck at the gaming tables had held, and his original stake was up to ninety thousand pounds. He planned to hand that to Feathers as a sign of good intent. But where did he come up with the rest?

The thought of getting out of town had occurred to him daily. But to return to Los Angeles seemed even more dangerous. He felt safer where he was.

He had telephoned Fontaine Khaled on three occasions and, even though he left messages, she never returned his calls. Not so much as a note to thank him for the diamond heart or the six dozen roses. Perhaps she was the bitch everyone said she was.

He had put her out of his mind, and concentrated on the tables.

Hal picked him up outside the Lamont at eight-thirty precisely.

'Nine o'clock meeting. We can't be late or early. Feathers is funny like that, so we'll play it safe and ride round the block when we get there.'

'Where does he live?' Nico asked.

'He never sees anyone at his home,' Hal explained. 'One of his Casinos is where we're meeting.'

☆

Fontaine surveyed herself in the full-length mirror one final time before leaving.

How could you beat perfection?

The long tube of black silk jersey, the blood red embroidered Chinese kimono, the Madam Butterfly hairdo. Startling, true, but very effective.

If she was in America now she would certainly appear on the front page of *Womens Wear Daily*.

She swept downstairs, and Mrs Walters was duly impressed. 'Oh, you do look lovely Mrs Khaled.'

Fontaine accepted the compliment as her due, and nodded regally. 'Is Ricky outside?'

'Yes, madam, and the Count is waiting in the living room.'

Oh God! The Count. She had forgotten about him. But then it certainly wouldn't have looked right if she had arrived at her own party without an escort.

Count Paulo waited impatiently. He leapt up when Fontaine entered the room.

'*Bellissimo! Bellissimo!*' he exclaimed.

'Calm down, sweetheart. Don't get yourself all excited.'

Who would have thought that she'd ever be bored by a twenty-five-year-old horny Italian Count? But she was. Indeed she was.

☆

Lynn met them at the reception desk. She acted like she had never set eyes on Nico before.

'Please follow me, gentlemen,' she said formally, 'Mr Feathers is expecting you.'

She led them through a door marked 'Private' which in turn led them through a narrow corridor.

'Great ass,' Hal managed to mutter as they followed Lynn.

She stopped at another door marked 'Private' and knocked three times.

A male voice called for them to come in.

They entered a luxurious office. Feathers sat behind an ornate desk. He was a big man with a taste for flashy suits and coloured shirts. His face was nightclub white and pasty, and his greased-down hair very obviously dyed black. In spite of the cheapness of his look he managed to throw out an aura of sinister and powerful menace.

He studied Nico through surprisingly small bloodshot eyes. Then he extended an even more surprising beautifully manicured hand, gave a dead fish kind of handshake and said, 'Take a seat, Nico. Hal, why don't you let Lynn take you for a walk?'

Hal quickly nodded, 'Sure, sure.'

Lynn directed a cold smile his way. 'Come along fat ass.' Her voice was as sensuous as ever. 'The big boys want to talk.'

She led Hal out of the room.

'Drink?' Feathers barked.

'Vodka, please.'

Feathers snapped his fingers, and a previously unnoticed hood stepped from the background and opened up a rather garish 1940s cocktail cabinet.

'Vodka,' snapped Feathers, 'and order me up a weak tea and some biscuits.'

The hood nodded obligingly. He looked like he belonged in the 1940s too.

'So,' Feathers sighed, 'you're Nico Constantine. I was interested to meet with a man who can play such a dangerous game with his life.'

Nico shrugged, 'I always intended to pay the Fonicettis back.'

'That's what they all say. Some of them even say it when their balls are decorating their ears, and their knee-caps are hanging by a thread.'

'You don't have to threaten me. I came here to try and work things out.'

'Good, Nico. Good. I'm glad.' Feathers leaned back in his chair. 'I understand that your luck at the tables has been remarkable since you've been in London.'

'Not that remarkable, but I can make a substantial deposit towards my debt.' He accepted a giant tumbler of neat vodka from the 1940s hood.

'Excellent. Of course, while you are in England your debt with the Fonicettis is my concern. We have a mutual agreement.'

Nico nodded. 'I understand that.'

'The Fonicettis were not thrilled by your sudden secretive departure. If only you had discussed things with them . . .'

Nico could feel himself getting irritated. He didn't like Feathers. He didn't like being lectured.

'Can you help me postpone the rest of the debt?' he asked abruptly.

'I can get you an extension,' Feathers said blandly. 'If you co-operate on a minor hustle.'

'What sort of hustle?'

'Nothing illegal . . . just slightly bent.' Then Feathers laughed, a particularly nasty laugh, 'Do you really feel you have a choice?' he asked.

'There is always a choice in life.' Nico replied shortly.

Feathers' small mean eyes darkened. 'Not for you. Not if you want to remain in good health.'

The tea arrived on a neat tray, with a selection of sweet biscuits.

Nico gulped a great slug of vodka. He had an insane desire to get out of there. 'What's the hustle?' he asked again.

'A certain horse is running in a big race next Saturday. This horse is the favourite, an out and out winner. What we want is the horse, to lose. What we want is for you to arrange it.'

Nico frowned. 'How can I do that?'

'The horse is called "Garbo". It belongs to Vanessa and Leonard Grant. The jockey, Sandy Roots, is giving a regular screwing to Mrs Grant – and while her husband might not mind – Sandy's wife would be more than put out. She's a lovely girl, daughter of top trainer, Charley Watson.' Feathers paused to dunk a biscuit in his tea. 'Now, if Charley got a whiff of what was going on . . . then Sandy may as well pack up and leave the business.'

'I don't understand,' Nico was puzzled. 'What does this all have to do with me?'

'Easy. Vanessa and Leonard Grant. Best friends of Fontaine Khaled.'

'So?'

'So we know all about you and Mrs Khaled. The plane. The night together.'

'We are no longer in touch.'

Feathers coughed. 'You'd better arrange to be. The Grants are having a house party this weekend. Mrs Khaled is already invited. So are the Roots, and Charley Watson. It will be easy for you to get an invite – you could fit right in with that lot.'

Nico hesitated, 'I don't know,' he said uncertainly. There was no way he wanted to use Fontaine Khaled again. Once was enough.

Feathers' tone was sharp. 'You join the weekend party, you persuade Sandy Roots to throw the race, and if you succeed . . . Well I am sure we can give you more time. Of course, if you don't succeed . . .' The menace was thick in Feathers' tone.

Nico had no choice but to agree.

☆

'Hobo' was packed when Fontaine made her entrance. Just like old times.

Steve Valentine rushed forward to greet her. He did look very effective all in white with his new hairstyle.

Sammy was doing a wonderful job of circulating, his natural warmth and friendliness appealing to everyone.

The new disc jockeys were wild, looning about in outrageous white satin outfits, and playing amazing sounds.

Even the waiters looked good in their new black and white uniforms.

'I love it!' Vanessa was already there. 'Sweetie, the atmosphere! It all makes "Dickies" seem rather old hat.'

'Do me a favour and dance with Paulo,' Fontaine hissed. 'He's boring the pants off me.'

'Is that a bad thing?'

'Oh, didn't I tell you? I've given up sex.'

'*You*?'

'Yes, me darling. Don't look so surprised.'

☆

'How did it go?' Hal asked.

Nico shrugged, 'Complicated. I don't want to involve you.'

Hal nodded, 'Suits me.'

'I have to see Fontaine,' Nico said.

'Business or pleasure?'

'Both.'

'You're in luck. It's the "Hobo" party tonight.'

'Let's go.'

They took a cab over. Nico wondered what the hell he was going to say to her. If it was any other female he would have had a whole line of stock phrases. But Fontaine . . . Well, she was different. Life could be very unfair at times.

☆

Fontaine was in her element. All the hard work of the previous days had been worth it. Everything was going right. She danced with various admirers, and thoroughly revelled in all the attention she was receiving.

Sammy was having as good a time as she was. Two sixteen-year-old groupies and a rock star were his personal guests.

Count Paulo hovered attentively wherever Fontaine went. 'Do take care of him,' she hissed in Vanessa's direction. But Vanessa was busying herself with a really boring, frighteningly short jockey, and his equally boring, rather tall wife.

Leonard invited Fontaine to dance. 'You are coming this weekend?' he asked anxiously as he jigged about in an embarrassing way.

'Of course. I could do with just lying about and relaxing.'

Leonard grinned. 'I can hardly imagine you relaxing.'

'Oh, I do, you'd be surprised.'

The frantic Wilson Pickett disco sound changed to a slow throbbing Donna Summer. Leonard seized his chance and grabbed her. His hands were hot and sweaty through her dress.

'A little looser, Leonard, I can't breathe.'

'What about lunch one day?'

'What about Vanessa?'

She managed to edge away. Horny husbands. She wished they would leave her alone.

☆

Hal had a date with a geriatric widow. He insisted on collecting her and bringing her to the 'Hobo' party.

Nico decided to fill him in on his conversation with Feathers, and Hal whistled and commented, 'Guess it's better than having your legs chopped off at the knees!'

Hal really knew how to make a person feel good.

They walked into 'Hobo', and it was all happening. The place was alive again. Excitement hung heavy in the air.

Sammy greeted them effusively, then insisted that they join his table in the discothèque.

Nico spotted Fontaine immediately. Other women paled beside her. She was an original. On the crowded dance floor she stood out.

Sammy was busy making introductions. Nico caught the name Sandy Roots, and he realized that he was practically sitting beside the jockey and his wife.

Hal pointedly tapped Nico on the arm. 'Have you met Vanessa Grant?' he asked.

Nico turned to the plumpish blonde woman and generated full wattage charm. 'My pleasure, madam.'

Vanessa sparkled. What more could she ask for? A magnetic stare from a very attractive stranger on one side. And her famous but rather short lover on the other.

Fontaine, returning from the dance floor, saw Nico, ignored him, and squeezed between Sandy Roots and the rock star.

Nico leaned across Vanessa. 'Good evening, Mrs Khaled.'

She pretended to notice him for the first time. 'Oh, Nico. How are you?' Her voice was cold, but suddenly her heart was racing like some stupid little teenager.

Count Paulo, sitting opposite her, said, 'Fontaine, we dance now?'

She dismissed him impatiently. 'In a minute, Paulo.'

'How have you been?' Nico inquired.

'Busy,' she replied.

At this point Vanessa got up to dance with Sandy Roots, and just as Count Paulo attempted to sit next to Fontaine, Nico moved up beside her, blocking him.

'You didn't return my calls,' Nico said softly.

'I told you, I've been busy.'

'You had no intention of returning my calls.'

'True.'

He reached out and touched the heart he had sent her, 'But you wear my heart.'

'It's pretty.'

'No – thank you?'

'Oh, I'm so sorry. Did I forget to say thank you like a good little girl?'

'You're still a bitch.'

'And you're still so fucking sure of yourself.'

'Why don't we get out of here? I want to talk to you properly.'

'There is nothing to talk about.'

'So, we'll make love. We both want to. Then, if you feel like it, we'll talk.'

He stood up, grabbed her firmly by the arm, and propelled her to the door.

She didn't protest. She didn't want to.

Count Paulo came running after them. 'Fontaine . . . Bellissimo – what is happening?'

'Go back inside, order a drink, and find someone of your own age to play with, sonny,' Nico said.

'But . . .' Paulo's mouth dropped open while he thought of something to say.

'Goodnight,' said Nico. And he and Fontaine exited up the stairs.

20

Dino bided his time for a week. He behaved as he always behaved. He dated a couple of showgirls, he wandered around the Casino with his usual Tony Curtis smile, he reported to his father every day.

As far as everyone connected to him could see, Cherry was just a distant memory, a slight brain storm. What had happened was in the past. Dino had been a naughty boy, and Joseph had rapped his knuckles. Now it was all over.

Or was it?

Beneath the Tony Curtis smile lurked an angry bitter man.

What his father had done to him was unforgivable. He had made a public fool of him. He had annulled his marriage as if he was some crazy teenager.

Dino would never forgive him for that.

☆

Joseph Fonicetti felt good. Everything taken care of. No loose ends. Even that bastard Nico had been found and warned.

Dino was a good son. A sensible boy. He had realized

the error of his ways. Dumb cunts were not for marrying. They were for humping out of your system.

☆

No way could Bernie marry Susanna again.

There were several reasons – the main one being that she would drive him fuckin' nuts!

She had a bossy streak that was to be believed. And nag nag constantly. And Daddy. And Starr, his own kid, a real little spoilt pain in the ass.

But how could he leave with the matter of Nico still unresolved?

It was impossible. He knew Susanna, she would go running straight to Carlos and blame the whole thing on him.

He sat in his office and pondered on what to do. The fifty thousand dollars was locked securely in his office safe, but he had not yet been able to contact Nico to offer his help.

His secretary walked into the office. She was a long-legged California blonde with lethal teeth.

She sat herself on the edge of his desk exhibiting an exciting length of leg. 'Your wife called.' she announced, 'while you were in the John. Wants you to call back right away.'

'She's not my wife, Tina.'

'Ex-wife. So what?'

That was the trouble with secretaries today. No fuckin' respect.

☆

'I'm flying to LA tomorrow morning,' Dino casually told Joseph.

'What for?' Joseph asked.

'The usual. Collect personally on a few of the outstanding markers.'

'Oh, yeah – yeah. Good.'

It was only acceptable to some of the Forum's more famous patrons to have their debts picked up by either Dino or David.

'I thought it was David's turn,' Joseph remarked.

'I'm doing him a favour. Mia's not feeling so good – only another six weeks' and you'll be a grandpop again.'

Joseph chuckled. David and Mia were doing well for him. A suitable few weeks' gap and he would ship in a prospective bride or two for Dino.

'Will you be staying over?' he asked.

'I don't know. Maybe, I'll let you know.'

Bright and early the next morning Dino was on a plane.

A car waited for him at LA airport. He knew exactly what he was going to do.

He wasn't nervous any more. He was suitably calm.

He was thirty-one years old and perfectly capable of making his own decisions.

Fuck Joseph Fonicetti and all he stood for. He, Dino, was going to be his own man. He wanted Cherry, and goddamnit he was going to have her.

☆

'Let's go upstairs,' Susanna suggested after dinner.

'I want to play some tapes over,' Bernie replied.

'You're becoming a real workaholic. Put the tapes on, switch the speakers through to the bedroom, and we'll listen to them together. OK?'

Her 'I wanna get laid' look was coming across loud and clear. 'They're long,' Bernie said desperately.

'That's fine. We've got all night, haven't we?'

'Sure.' Suddenly he was a sex object. *Her* sex object. Something was wrong somewhere.

'So, come on, Bernie. Do it, what are you waiting for?' She winked, and walked ahead of him up the stairs.

☆

Dino parked outside Cherry's apartment building. He hadn't wanted to phone her, after all, her first reaction might not be exactly friendly. He hadn't dared to call her from Vegas – he wouldn't put it past Joseph to have a tap on his phone.

The apartment house was slightly on the seedy side. Peeling paintwork and garbage cans right out front where you could see them.

The communal pool had rotten tiles, and dilapidated lounging chairs around it.

Dino was used to luxurious surroundings, always had been. He turned up his nose in distaste at the various cooking smells. It was a shame that delectable Cherry had to live in such a sordid place. It stank of failure and survival on the lowest level.

Oh well, he would soon be taking her away from all this.

He found her apartment number and pressed the buzzer. No answer. So he tried again.

A faded redhead with enormous tits and a sackful of cat droppings emerged from the next-door apartment.

'Hi,' she said, looking Dino over appreciatively.

'Do you know if anybody's home?' he asked.

'Shouldn't think so. Those little ladies keep themselves *veree* busy. Know what I mean, buster?' She smiled broadly, forgetting the fact that she had not put her two front false teeth in.

Dino was surprised that Cherry lived with room-mates. She certainly had never mentioned them.

'Wanna come in for a coffee, honey?' the redhead leered.

Dino threw her a cold stare.

'Only trying to be neighbourly, dear. Hey,' she peered at him closely, 'anyone ever tell you that you look like Tony Curtis?'

A commotion heralded the arrival of one of Cherry's room-mates. She was a very tall girl, accompanied by two large alsatian dogs, a lot of fishing tackle, suitcases, and her porno movie star boyfriend who looked like Mr Universe.

The redhead sniffed and vanished quickly inside her apartment, cat droppings and all.

'Lookin' for someone?' the girl demanded, while the two alsatians sniffed around his crotch.

Dino tried to shove them away.

'Watch it,' Mr Universe porno movie star said in a falsetto voice.

'Jesus Christ!' the girl exclaimed for no particular reason.

'Is Cherry around?' Dino asked.

'I dunno. I've been away. For crissakes open up the door.'

Mr Universe struggled with the key, and the three of them entered the apartment.

'What the fuck's that Godawful smell?' The girl exclaimed. 'Cherry? You around? There's some guy here for you.'

Dino backed towards the door. He didn't like the apartment. He didn't like the occupants. He didn't like the whole set up.

'Shit!' the girl said.

She was certainly no Cherry. More like a tough little hooker.

'You. wanna hang around?' she asked unenthusiastically.

'Gotta take a piss,' Mr Universe announced.

A really lovely couple.

'No,' said Dino, 'I think I'll come back later.'

'Suit yourself,' the girl shrugged. 'You leavin' a message?'

'Sheeiit! Jeez!' Mr Universe's falsetto tones screamed out. 'Get in here, get in here quick.'

The girl and Dino and the two alsatians rushed into the bathroom.

Cherry lay in the bath – quite quite dead.

☆

Susanna woke early, fixed a big pitcher of orange juice, and went into her study to work on the design for the wedding invitations.

She hummed softly to herself. It was quite nice having Bernie around the house again. Only quite.

He was as neurotic as ever. He picked his nose all over her special lavender sheets. He sulked a lot. And he was still jealous of daddy.

However . . . he *was* pretty nifty in bed. He could do more with his tongue than a whole legion of upstanding pricks.

Susanna giggled to herself .

The phone rang and she picked it up.

An incoherent babbling voice was screaming at the other end.

'Who is this?' she demanded.

It was Dino.

☆

By the time Bernie got up, Dino was already at the house.

Susanna had him comparatively calmed down and coherent.

It must have been shock enough for him to find Cherry's body, but the fact that the girl had lain in a bath filled with her own blood for a week . . .

She had slit her wrists.

Dino had run from the apartment at once. But not before he had been forced to take a good look. 'Christ, Susy, it was the most horrible sight of my whole life,' he babbled.

Susanna comforted him. She fed him brandy, held him, and stroked his forehead. She and Dino had known each other all their lives. When she was thirteen she had developed a big crush on him that had lasted all of six months.

They had made love once, and ever since that time remained close friends.

'I thought of you immediately,' Dino said. 'I mean you and Bernie knew Cherry . . .' He broke off into sobs.

Bernie couldn't believe the news. Cherry. Killed herself. Why? It was such a waste.

He thought of Nico. Knew he would blame himself, and decided not to tell him.

'Dino, I want you to stay here,' Susanna insisted. 'You need the rest, I'll call Uncle Joseph.'

Gratefully Dino accepted her hospitality. He had a nagging gut ache and he knew why. Something was bothering him.

Had Cherry taken her own life?

Or – had his father arranged it?

It was something he would never know. But it would certainly be a long time before he went back to the family business.

21

Ricky drove the Rolls. Eyes straight ahead. Face impassive.

He had a feeling that his days were numbered as Mrs Khaled's chauffeur. Ever since their one drunken evening together she had become frostier and frostier. Never once had she mentioned it. He was beginning to think that maybe it had never even happened!

Of course he had told Polly all about it, thinking that she would enjoy the juicy details. Wrong. Polly had listened, asked questions, pursed her lips, and never allowed him into her bed again.

Women were funny creatures.

They were approaching the driveway of the Grants' country estate. Very impressive. Parked casually outside the front entrance of the mansion were two Ferraris, a Bentley, and a Lamborghini.

'We're here, Nico,' Fontaine exclaimed. 'You're going to love the house.'

He held her hand and squeezed it tightly. 'I'm sure I will.'

Fontaine was positively glowing. She even looked different – softer and more relaxed, her biting edginess in abeyance.

Leonard came out to greet them.

He kissed Fontaine and gave Nico a quizzical onceover. 'A little old for you, isn't he?' he murmured discreetly to Fontaine.

'Leonard, I think I'm finally growing up.'

'Really, How boring. I hope he's rich at least.'

'Naturally. But that's *not* the reason I'm with him.'

Leonard nodded knowingly.

Nico, meanwhile, was organizing the suitcases from the trunk of the car.

'Good God!' Leonard exclaimed, noticing all their luggage. 'You're only here for the weekend!'

Fontaine smiled. 'You should know me by now, I just can't stand to look tacky, and Nico's exactly the same. We're soulmates.' She gave Nico a very long and intimate look. 'Aren't we darling?'

'You could put it like that.' His eyes locked with hers.

'I will put it like that.'

Their eyes carried on a secret conversation.

Leonard stamped his feet impatiently. 'Shall we go inside?' he suggested.

Fontaine broke the look. 'Wonderful. Who is here?'

'Susan and Sandy Roots, my trainer – Charley Watson. Pearson Crichton-Stuart, and a most delightful little Chinese piece.'

'Got your eye on her already, Leonard?' Fontaine mocked.

'Not at all.'

Fontaine suddenly turned her stare to Ricky. 'You can leave the car,' she said brusquely. 'Take the train back to town. I won't be needing you again this weekend.'

Ricky nodded. He had made a decision. The randy Mrs Khaled could stuff her chauffeur's job. He was quitting.

'Yes, Mrs Khaled.' Bitch!

☆

The weekend got off to a good start. Everyone seemed to get along well.

Nico watched Sandy Roots carefully. He seemed a nice enough lad, but Nico did not miss the secret glances passing like fire between him and Vanessa at lunch.

After lunch Fontaine wanted to go riding. 'Can we?' she asked Nico.

'I don't feel like it,' he replied. 'But you go.'

'Come on, old girl,' Leonard said. '*I'll* take you. Anyone else want to come?'

'I wish you wouldn't call me "old girl",' Fontaine snapped. 'Nico, are you sure you won't come?'

'I feel like a game or two of backgammon, if I can interest anyone.'

Pearson Crichton-Stuart piped up with, 'Me, I'm rather good at the game actually.'

Nico winked at Fontaine. 'Then we shall play for stakes, don't you think? Makes the game more interesting.'

Fontaine kissed him on the forehead. 'I'm going to change. I'll see you later.' She bent, and whispered in his ear, 'Hustler!'

'You bet!' he replied.

While she was changing she thought about their relationship. Nico was the most exciting, interesting, attractive man she had ever met. After all the boys – here was a real man. And yet he was also mysterious, and she liked that too. She had a horrible feeling that for the first time in her life she was in love. God forbid!

Downstairs Leonard waited for her, and they set off for the stables in a Land-Rover.

'I hope you've bet your all on our horse tomorrow,' Leonard commented. 'In all my years involved with racing I've never seen form like it.'

'Yes, Vanessa told me. I've placed a few very substantial bets.'

'Good girl.'

She didn't want to elaborate and tell him that she had her house and car riding on it. She needed a big win.

☆

Nico trounced Pearson at backgammon twice, but still he came back for more.

His tiny Chinese girlfriend – Mai-Ling – watched attentively.

Charley Watson snored, asleep in front of the roaring log fire. Susan Roots had gone out shopping.

Nico was the only one that noticed Vanessa and Sandy slip quietly away.

Riding through the wooded grounds was very exhilarating. Fontaine threw her head back and enjoyed the wind tearing through her hair. Terrible for the complexion of course. But so what . . .

'Let's take a rest,' Leonard shouted.

They dismounted in a clearing, and before Fontaine even had time to think, Leonard was all over her.

She tried to push him off. 'What *do* you think you're doing?' she asked sharply.

Leonard pulled at her clothes. 'You want it . . . You can't fool me . . . this is your scene . . .'

Fontaine found herself struggling with him in earnest. 'Leonard. For crissakes stop it.'

'You like it . . . you want it . . . I've always fancied you, Fontaine, and don't you deny it. You've always fancied me, too.'

He was tearing viciously at her clothes now.

She couldn't believe what was happening. With a violent kick she managed to throw him off her, but it was too late to stop him having an orgasm.

He rolled on the ground groaning in ectasy and pain.

Fontaine got up quickly. 'You filthy bastard!' she hissed.

She mounted her horse and rode back to the house, seething with fury.

Nico was still playing backgammon and taking a bundle off the rather chinless Pearson Crichton-Stuart.

'I want to leave,' Fontaine stormed.

Nico didn't take his eyes from the board. 'Why?'

Fontaine couldn't think of a reason. The truth was too humiliating.

'I just feel like going home.'

'No,' said Nico firmly. 'We'll stay for the big race tomorrow, *then* we'll go home.'

Fontaine had to admit that one of the things she loved

about Nico was that he did what he wanted to – not what she told him to.

It made a very acceptable change.

☆

Dinner that evening was a formal affair. Vanessa had decided it would be fun to dress up.

Nico was in high spirits. He had managed to take over two thousand pounds off Pearson Crichton-Stuart.

'It's just not done,' Fontaine chided him gently in the privacy of their room before dinner. 'Let the poor fellow win some of it back later.'

Nico laughed. 'You're so English! He wanted to gamble. He lost. That's all there is to it.' For a moment he was tempted to tell her of his gambling debts and everything else. But he curbed the temptation. She would probably be horrified. And worse – she would probably offer to bail him out. And he didn't want her money. Although a couple of her diamond rings would no doubt raise enough to solve all of his problems. One lady who would *never* be caught dead in fake gems was Mrs Khaled.

The opportunity to talk to Sandy Roots in private was not easy to obtain. Nico finally cornered him after dinner. He hated what he had to do, but then again, he had no choice. He engaged the young jockey in a this and that conversation about racing. Then he sprung the surprise. At first Sandy pretended not to know what Nico was talking about. Then, at last, he realized that Nico meant business. And of course, in the end, he had to agree. He was just about smart enough to know that his racing career could well be over if Charley Watson wanted it that way. And if Charley Watson found out that he was screwing Vanessa Grant . . . He would definitely want it that way. No doubt on *that* score.

'I'll do it,' he finally agreed. 'But I don't know how a lousy bastard like you can sleep at nights.'

Nico felt like a lousy bastard. Sandy was right.

Pearson Crichton-Stuart was bugging him for another game of backgammon.

Fontaine gave him a warning look.

He blew her a kiss.

'Don't forget to lose,' she mouthed.

'Never!' Nico mouthed back.

'What do you think of Sandy?' Vanessa whispered to Fontaine.

'Sandy?' Fontaine questioned vaguely. 'Oh, you mean the little jockey chap.'

Vanessa rolled her eyes meaningfully. 'Not so little!'

Fontaine didn't catch the drift of what she was trying to tell her at all. She was too busy directing icy stares at Leonard, across the room.

'Leonard's getting fat,' she snapped. 'Why don't you send him away to a health farm?'

'Do you think so?'

'Yes, I do. He's at a dangerous age. True heart attack material.'

'Oh, no!' Vanessa was anxious.

'Oh, yes,' Fontaine replied coldly, 'He's looking positively *old*.'

'I like Nico,' Vanessa changed the subject. 'I've never seen you so . . .'

'Hooked?'

Vanessa giggled. 'It does seem that way.'

Fontaine smiled. 'Yes. And to tell you the truth, I'm loving every minute of it.'

☆

The day of the big race everyone got up early. It was crisp and cold, but the sun was shining.

Vanessa served a buffet breakfast with the help of three servants.

'This is *delicious*!' Fontaine exclaimed. 'I haven't had kippers for simply years!'

Nico picked up a copy of *Sporting Life* and started studying the form. Since 'Garbo' would definitely not be winning the big race he may as well check out the other runners.

He found a real outsider. A French horse called 'Kanga'. Twenty-five to one. The odds were right, so he decided to phone Hal and find out the form.

Hal was encouraging. He knew of the horse. It had come second in a race earlier in the season. Since then – nothing. But the early form was promising, and if the weather conditions were right . . .

'I want to place my bankroll on it,' Nico said.

'What bankroll?' Hal laughed.

'I held ten thou back when I paid Feathers. I want you to get on to two or three bookies and place it for me. But not until just before the race. I want to keep those odds.'

'It's a gamble,' Hal warned.

'Ah,' replied Nico. 'But isn't that what life is all about?'

22

Bernie was the last to realize what was going on. And when he found out he was the most grateful.

It all started very innocently. Dino moving in with them. Susanna consoling him day and night – sometimes very late into the night. And Susanna suddenly Miss Sweetness and Light. No nagging. No mention of wedding plans. And certainly no sex.

When Bernie thought about it after, he realized what a dumb schmuck he must have seemed to both of them. He almost laughed out loud when he thought of the Dear John scene. It went as follows.

They had dined, the three of them. Then Bernie had gone into his study to play some tapes, and Susanna and Dino had stayed in the dining room chatting intently.

An hour later, they had presented themselves to him, hand in hand.

He hadn't even thought twice about *that*.

'Bernie, we have to talk to you,' Susanna said. 'Make yourself a stiff drink and sit down.'

Christ! Nico! The sons-of-bitches had done something to Nico.

'I don't need to sit down and have a drink. What the fuck is going on?'

Susanna had come to him then. Comforting hand on the arm, maternal cluck-clucking sounds coming from the lips.

'I knew you'd be upset, Bernie. But *please, please*, for all of us, try to understand.'

'Understand *what* for crissakes?' He was roaring with anger.

'Dino and I want to get married,' Susanna said simply.

'What?' He couldn't believe his ears. Or his luck.

'I know it must be hard for you, but we fought it, we really did, and then . . .' She shrugged helplessly. 'We knew we had to tell you.'

Bernie wanted to laugh out loud.

Susanna and Dino. What a pair! And Joseph and Carlos would be celebrating for weeks – months even.

Bernie forced his face into a suitably miserable expression.

Dino said smoothly, 'I know it's tough, but Jeez – it's hit us both like a ton of bricks.'

A ton of shit more like.

'I'm confused . . .' Bernie managed to mumble.

'Yes. You must be,' said Susanna, her voice becoming more businesslike. 'The thing is, Bernie, I think you should move back into that house you were sharing with Nico.'

Oh, sure. Get rid of him immediately.

'We've discussed everything,' Susanna said. 'And we all know how close you and Nico are.'

She made them sound like a couple of closet queens!

'So,' Dino continued, 'we've decided to allow Nico more time to pay. I've spoken to my father about it and he's agreed. Three months. But that's the limit.'

It was a swop. Bernie move out of Susanna's life with no fuss and bother, and Nico would get more time.

'How about six months?' Bernie ventured.

'Forget it,' Dino snapped.

'They're being very fair,' Susanna said, in her new Florence Nightingale voice.

So Bernie had moved out. What an escape!

He phoned Nico in London immediately with the good news, but the hotel operator at the Lamont said that Mr Constantine was away for the weekend and would be returning on Monday.

Oh, well, the good news would just have to wait.